BUFFALO RUN

BUFFALO RUN

WALT COBURN

THORNDIKE
CHIVERS

This Large Print edition is published by Thorndike Press®, Waterville, Maine USA and by BBC Audiobooks, Ltd, Bath, England.

Published in 2004 in the U.S. by arrangement with Golden West Literary Agency.

Published in 2004 in the U.K. by arrangement with Golden West Literary Agency.

U.S. Hardcover 0-7862-6217-6 (Western)
U.K. Hardcover 0-7540-9941-5 (Chivers Large Print)
U.K. Softcover 0-7540-9942-3 (Camden Large Print)

The text of this Large Print edition is unabridged.
Other aspects of the book may vary from the original edition.

Set in 16 pt. Plantin by Minnie B. Raven.

Printed in the United States on permanent paper.

British Library Cataloguing-in-Publication Data available

Library of Congress Cataloging-in-Publication Data

Coburn, Walt, 1889–1971.
    Buffalo run / Walt Coburn.
        p. cm.
    ISBN 0-7862-6217-6 (lg. print : hc : alk. paper)
    1. Montana — Fiction. 2. Sects — Fiction. 3. Large type books. I. Title.
PS3505.O153B84 2004
813'.52—dc22   2003068657

BUFFALO RUN

CHAPTER ONE

Bryce Bradford had ridden a long way. He was seeing the little cow town of Buffalo Run, Montana, far the first time after a heavy rain when the clouds had cleared and the sky was a sapphire blue and the muddy ground steaming.

The hitchracks along the street were lined with saddled horses and teams hitched to buckboards or wagons. Most of the buildings were saloons, except for a trading store, an assay office and a two-storied hotel. There was a large warehouse at the end of the street.

Bryce had taken off his fringed chaps and they hung from his saddlehorn in front of his long legs. His California pants were new, with an Indian-tanned white buckskin seat sewn into the heavy wool. He wore a six-shooter in a holster tied to his thigh. He was clean-shaven, his features clear and strong. His hair was heavy and black.

As he sat his horse deciding whether to dismount or take his horse to the feed barn and corrals at the edge of town, he heard a

7

woman's voice cry out, in anger rather than fear. Bryce spurred his horse towards the boardwalk when he saw the girl struggling to free herself from the manhandling of a flashily dressed man whom Bryce spotted for a gambler. He was trying to drag the protesting girl into the El Dorado Saloon.

Bryce quit his saddle with a quick, easy swing. He jerked the man around by his coat collar, then landed a hard, open-handed slap to the face.

The man jerked free. His hand slid under his coat and came out with a snub-barrelled gun, the type carried by gamblers and known as a belly-gun.

Bryce's six-shooter was in his hand with an unbroken movement, spewing a streak of flame. The gambler's gun roared but the shot went wild as his knees buckled and he crumpled in a heap.

Bryce picked the girl up and swung her into the saddle, then vaulted up behind her, spurring his horse to a run.

'Whichaway, ma'am?' he asked.

'Past the barn, then turn right. You killed him, didn't you?'

'I didn't shoot to miss, ma'am.' Bryce's voice was tense, unsteady. The girl's thick copper-colored hair was in his face and when she turned her head he saw that her grey eyes were dark with fear and her tanned cheeks pale.

They were headed across a strip of land covered with tall buffalo grass, following a trail that led to a sod-roofed log cabin. As they approached, a gaunt man in a white shirt and baggy trousers came out. His mop of iron-grey hair was untidy and he was swaying a little unsteadily.

'Well, well, daughter, who is this gallant blade? Judge Plato Morgan welcomes you, sir. . . .'

'Please, father! We're . . . he's in trouble . . . he told me his name was Bryce Bradford, a stranger in town. He just shot Charlie Decker, the gambler!'

'In that case, my hospitality increases a hundredfold. My legal advice is at your service, sir.'

Bryce slid to the ground and lifted the girl down. Her smile was strained. Obviously her father was a little drunk. Her sunbonnet hung from her throat and the top of her head came below the level of Bryce's shoulder, so that she had to tilt her face up to look at him.

There was a strange fear, almost loathing, in her eyes as she backed away from him. Her hands were clenched into small

9

fists as she spoke, 'You just killed a man. Take my advice and leave Buffalo Run right now. And never come back!'

Her face was drained of color, her eyes glazed with horror. It was as if she were accusing herself of having taken part in the killing. She kept staring at him as if he were a vicious animal that killed wantonly.

Bryce felt the slow anger and resentment chilling his insides. Instead of thanking him, this girl was blaming him for shooting a man in self-defense, accusing him of rank murder. She had gotten him into it and now she wanted him to run off like a coyote.

He had just killed a man, just missed sudden death by inches. He had undone all his careful planning to lose himself and his identity in Montana. He was in a tight and there was no chance to run, even if he wanted to. Buffalo Run was a prairie town. For miles in every direction the country was flat, with rolling hills and distant high benchlands. The nearest rough country that would afford a hideout were the distant blue Highwood Mountains and the badlands along the Missouri river, a long hard day's ride on a fresh horse.

The girl's father said he'd bring a jug and some glasses from the cabin, but

Bryce didn't wait for him to come out again. He stepped up on his horse and rode away without a backward glance.

The sun had gone down and the shadows of dusk were covering the prairie, grey and threatening as the danger that lay in wait for him at Buffalo Run.

As he approached the town he could tell that a posse was being organized. Men on horseback were waiting in front of the El Dorado where the gambler still lay sprawled on the boardwalk where he had died.

Bryce Bradford was a stranger in a strange land. So far as he knew he hadn't a single acquaintance or friend to take his part.

A dozen or more men had been eye witness to the killing in self-defense. They had seen the whole play from start to finish. Bryce kept telling himself to bolster his courage, but the chill of dread was pinching his belly when he rode at a walk up the main street, noticing that the men on horseback sat their saddles with hands on their guns and that three men stood apart from the milling crowd to block his approach.

Bryce halted in front of them. A hush had fallen over the crowd, a tense, dangerous silence. Bryce's two hands rested on the saddlehorn and he met their cold scrutiny with steady eyes. The tall, black-clad man, Bryce thought, would be the one most likely to make a gun play so he kept his eyes on him, ready to pull his gun and play it out to a swift deadly finish. He tried not to let them see that he was quivering inside as they measured him with cold appraisal.

'Get off your horse, Stranger,' the tall dangerous looking one said.

Bryce dismounted. Someone took his horse.

Bryce followed the three men into the saloon and down a narrow hallway to a room that was perhaps fifteen-feet square, furnished with a large round green-covered cardtable and half a dozen heavy chairs. A bartender wearing a soiled white apron followed them in with a whisky bottle and glasses which he set on the table, then departed.

One of the men closed and bolted the door. They all sat down.

Bryce could hear the clumping of boots in the hall and figured the room must be guarded. The one window was painted with layers of blackish green to make it opaque. The only light was a swinging lamp over the cardtable.

Bryce told them his name when they asked him. The tall black-clad man identified himself and his two companions, saying, 'I'm Jack Quensel. I own the El Dorado Saloon. Tim Fogarty here owns some freight outfits and operates the Wells Fargo Express from Buffalo Run to Fort Benton. Pete Kaster is a mining and cattle man.'

The whisky bottle was passed but Bryce noticed that Quensel did not take a drink. He had a sallow face that did not change expression and a drooping black moustache concealed the barest smile of contempt for his two companions. His opaque black eyes kept sizing Bryce up.

Tim Fogarty was a large man, all hard muscle and big bone. His fiery red hair was tossed around his roughly hewn face, his green eyes blazed. Bryce figured he'd be a hard man to whip in a fight.

Pete Kaster was short and barrel chested, with bowed legs. He wore the rough clothes of a cowman and his greying black hair and beard needed trimming. Bryce didn't like what he saw in the man.

It was Jack Quensel who said, 'As a committee of three representing the Stranglers of Buffalo Run, we find you guilty of the murder of Charlie Decker. Witnesses have been questioned who agree that you first struck Decker, then when he drew his gun, you shot him. Have you anything to say for yourself, Bryce Bradford?'

But before Bryce could answer in his own defense, the raised voice of Judge Plato Morgan could be heard out in the hall. He was demanding entrance.

'Let the old rascal in', chuckled Tim Fogarty. 'I'll get him to recite "Osler Joe" or the one about Casey at the Bat. Get him likkered and he's better'n your stage shows, Quensel.'

Before Quensel could offer protest, Pete Kaster had pulled back the bolt and opened the door.

Judge Morgan had on a black coat, a black Confederate army hat and a hastily tied black string tie. He carried a gold-headed ebony cane like a sabre.

He strode in, his gait steadier than it had been at the cabin. Pete Kaster closed and bolted the door.

'Drink, Judge?' suggested Tim Fogarty.

The judge declined. He said, 'I am here to demand justice for this young man. His was an honorable deed in defense of my daughter's honor. He shot that blackleg tinhorn only after Decker pulled his gun first.'

'Bryce Bradford has just been tried by a committee of three representing the Stranglers', Quensel spoke up quickly. 'We found him guilty!'

'Have a drink, Judge,' interrupted Tim Fogarty, 'then give us "The Face on the Bar-room Floor"!'

'Hah! You mock a man who stands before you in the name of justice. You, Fogarty, a foul tongued bull-whacker, and your illiterate partner, Pete Kaster, who jumps the mining claims of honest prospectors, and you, Quensel, a man who fills his coffers with the ill-gotten gains derived from this den of iniquity.

'Who among you is fit to condemn this man who within the hour has rid the earth of as unmitigated a villain as ever tainted the clear air with foul breath?

'I demand that my client be set free!' Judge Plato Morgan paused, out of breath.

'In that case,' Jack Quensel's flat voice fell across the last echoes of Morgan's speech, 'I think the case should be dismissed.'

'Hah! By God. . . . !'

'Just one minute Morgan', said Quensel. 'Bryce Bradford will not be allowed to leave town until his case is dismissed by a two-thirds vote of the Stranglers, at their next meeting.'

Jack Quensel's cold black eyes were fixed on Bryce now. He said, 'Give us your word that you'll not try to leave town, it won't be necessary to lock you up, Bradford.'

'I give you my word', Bryce answered quickly.

'Where did you come from, Bradford?' Quensel shot the question.

'My past history is my own business.' Bryce was suddenly on guard.

'Right as hell!' chuckled Tim Fogarty. He filled a glass and shoved it into the judge's hand. 'A fine speech, Judge,' he said, 'even if you did call us names. Now if you'll give us that one about Lasca, we'll call 'er a day.'

Judge Morgan twirled his glass of whisky and smiled. It was good whisky.

'To Bryce Bradford,' he bowed stiffly, 'Gentlemen!' He swallowed his drink thirstily. Before he could set down the empty glass, Fogarty had it filled again.

Judge Plato Morgan was reciting poems at the long well-patronized bar when Bryce went out through the swinging half doors.

A cowpuncher's first thought concerns the welfare of the horse that packs him. Bryce headed for the feed and livery barn

16

at the end of the street. Blobs of yellow light from the row of saloons fell across the plank sidewalk and reflected on the puddles of muddy water on the wide, wheel-rutted deserted street.

A cold white half moon rode through the stars. The men were all inside the saloons, gathered for the most part at the El Dorado where a sort of wake for the dead gambler and part owner of the place was in progress.

The clump of Bryce's boot-heels made a mocking echo in his ears. Then he stepped off the sidewalk into the sticky gumbo. He stopped just inside the lantern lit barn to scrape the mud from his boots with a manure-fork.

He found his horse in a stall, the manger filled with fresh wild hay cut on the prairie. He began reading the brand on each horse in the barn. He paused at a double stall that held a bay and a sorrel, and his jaw muscles tightened as he read the identical brands on the left thigh of each saddle-horse. His hand instinctively dropped to the butt of his gun and he looked around almost furtively.

He wondered how many men in Montana knew that Square and Compass brand that belonged down in Utah. It branded some of the world's finest horses, bred to mount that grim and secret band of men known as the Avenging Angels of the Mormon Church.

The door of the saddle and harness room was kicked open. The grizzled barnman came limping out on saddle-warped rheumatic legs. Bryce stepped out from between the two Square and Compass horses. He asked the barnman who owned the two mounts.

'One was a big rawboned feller with grey hair and a spade beard,' the barnman told him as he hooked up his suspenders. 'The younger one was the spittin' image of his old man except that he was cross-eyed. They paid two weeks' feed bill in advance. Bought two of the best grain fed saddle-horses Tim Fogarty had and pulled out. That was a week ago.'

'They say what fetched them to Buffalo Run?'

'Neither one of 'em said a word. When the spade beard feller looked at you, you plumb forgot whatever it was you were going to ask him. If ever I seen a pair of killers, and I've seen plenty tough men in my day, that old man and his son had the brand on their hides.'

The old man's puckered eyes squinted.

He took a gnawed plug of tobacco from his pocket and bit off a piece, tonguing it into his cheek before he spoke. 'If you need a fresh horse, son, Old Dad Jones will go back to bed and know nothin' if one of them Square and Compass geldings is missin'.'

Bryce Bradford shook his head and grinned his thanks. 'I have to stand a Strangler trial for the murder of Charlie Decker. Judge Morgan is my lawyer. I gave Quensel my word not to leave Buffalo Run.'

'Listen, son,' Dad Jones lowered his voice in a confidential whisper, 'Quensel is the law here. A group of his followers known as the Stranglers are a disgrace to the Montana Vigilantes such as you'll find at Virginia City and Fort Benton. They're a pack of murderers.'

'What about Judge Plato Morgan?' Bryce inquired.

'The Judge likes his likker along with a little game of cards. He likes to spout poems. He had considerable money when he stopped overnight here about a year ago; got drunk and gambled it all away. Quensel gave him the position of Justice of the Peace. The job turned out to be judge of a kangaroo court.'

'He lives with his proud daughter Virginia in a sod roofed log cabin. Sometimes they don't have enough to eat.' Dad Jones spat tobacco juice on the dirt floor.

'I'll be around about then', Dad Jones told him. 'I ain't so old but what I can still handle that ol' hawglaig I got in my warsack.'

'No need in you getting messed up in a gun ruckus, Dad.'

The old man chuckled. 'That Virginia Morgan is worth fightin' for.'

'She backs away from me like I had smallpox,' Bryce said.

'Like as not she never saw a man shot down. You can't blame her for shyin' off from a man she's just watched kill another man. Give her time to get over the shock. One of these days she'll realize you killed Decker on her account and she'll come runnin' to thank you.'

'One of these days I won't be here, Dad. If my luck holds out I'll be driftin' yonderly. There's no place for a girl like Virginia Morgan along the trail I'll be travellin'.'

'On account of those two Square and Compass killers?'

'That's right, Dad,' Bryce answered, his heavy brows pulled into a thoughtful scowl. 'I better show back at the El Dorado before they send for me.'

'Watch your step, son. I'll be around if I'm needed.'

CHAPTER TWO

Jack Quensel, Big Tim Fogarty and Pete Kaster were holding a meeting behind a bolted, guarded door.

'He's our man,' said Quensel. 'Bryce Bradford is made to order for the job.'

'What makes you think he'll string along with us?' growled Fogarty.

'We'll vote him in as sheriff and we'll elect that old rum-soaked Plato Morgan as judge. Buffalo Run will have law and order.'

'We've been getting along so far,' protested Pete Kaster, 'without much trouble. What's the sense of electing a sheriff and a judge?'

'We've gotten along so far,' said Quensel flatly, 'by wiping out any man that looked like he might give us trouble. If you think we're not skating on thin ice, just study the letter that would have gone to the Wells Fargo Express headquarters at Fort Benton if Decker hadn't shot that man I spotted for a detective yesterday.

'I got the letter out of Decker's pocket. It's got his blood on it. Decker, unless I'm badly mistaken, was holding it with some idea of double-crossing us.' Quensel reached into his pocket and produced the letter. 'I'll read it aloud,' he told them. 'Listen carefully.'

To the Wells Fargo Agent,
Fort Benton, Montana
Confidential.

My investigation here has proven beyond all doubt that the frequent holding up of the stage and robbing the mail and Wells Fargo Express shipments of gold, etc., has been the work of one man. His name is Charlie Decker. Decker is simply a tool in the hands of more dangerous men who have hired him to do the actual road-agent work. The stage driver is in the employ of Big Tim Fogarty and is paid to keep his mouth shut. The shotgun messengers you have hired were either intimidated or bought off by Fogarty, Jack Quensel and Peter Kaster. One or two who couldn't be bribed or scared off were murdered.

Fogarty, Quensel and Kaster are the organizers of the Stranglers here at Buffalo Run. Even Decker is a member of that secret organization supposed to uphold law and order. Few, if any, of the Stranglers are aware that they are being hoodwinked by the three leaders. When any man begins to suspect the truth, that man is murdered. I will be fortunate if I am allowed to leave here alive. Decker suspects me. He has tried to get me drunk in order to loosen my tongue. He has made me a secret proposition to double-cross Quensel, Fogarty and Kaster. I am leading him on cautiously, in hopes of obtaining definite proof we need.

This letter is to keep you informed as to my activities. It may be my own death warrant I am writing. In case I am killed, these three men will have hired Decker to do the actual job.

I will mail this at the first opportunity or send it by some messenger I can trust. Though it is hard to find a man in Buffalo Run. . . .

'The letter,' smiled Quensel, 'was never finished. Decker walked into the detective's room and shot him. He didn't hand over the letter for some reason. I think he had some plan to sell us down the river. Bryce Bradford did us one hell of a big favor when he killed Decker.'

Quensel folded the letter and put it in his inside coat pocket. The face of each man showed that they were badly disturbed.

'So,' Quensel said, his eyes watching his two companions closely, 'we need to change tactics. What that long-nosed detective learned before I paid Decker five hundred dollars to rub him out, other men must suspect. We'll be strung up by our own Stranglers unless we act right now. And our surest, safest bet is to do an about face.

'A dozen or more men saw Bryce Bradford kill Decker. Most of them distrusted Decker. They saw the stranger play the big hero. Nominate him for sheriff and they'll yell three cheers till they're hoarse as a flock of crows. Sheriff Bryce Bradford is a cinch bet.'

'Supposin' he's honest?' Fogarty's red brows knit in a scowl. 'He don't look easy to handle, Quensel.'

'I've got an ace in the hole, my friend. I'm keeping it buried till I need to play it. I don't back losers.'

'Bryce Bradford,' growled Pete Kaster, 'is as safe as a black powder keg next to a red-hot stove. If we got to have a sheriff here at Buffalo Run, let's put in a man we can handle.'

'And be in no better fix than we are now. We've got to put in a man who can't be bought or scared off. Buffalo Run is going to have an honest sheriff. When the time comes, I'll handle Bradford. I'm calling a meeting of the Stranglers tonight at midnight.'

'All right, Quensel,' agreed Fogarty reluctantly. 'But what about this electing Morgan for judge? Ain't he cussed the three of us out? For all his drunken poetry spoutin', that old coot has more fire an' brimstone in him than a camp meetin' preacher. If ever we get up before him, he'll have us swingin' from a cottonwood limb!'

'Sure,' smiled Quensel, 'Morgan is going to take his job seriously but don't forget that he's the biggest drunkard in Buffalo Run. He gambled away every dollar he had when he came a year ago. He's a bar-room bum. He and his daughter are practically living on charity right now. She was on her way to keep an appointment with me regarding a job when Decker made that clumsy play that sent him to hell. I'll handle the Judge and his daughter, gentlemen. I may even marry the girl.'

Tim Fogarty's big hairy hand clenched, showing a gold ring mounted with the biggest diamond in Montana, his bloodshot eyes glared at the suave, handsome gambler. He said, 'Stick to your honkeytonk wenches, Quensel. Bother Virginia Morgan and I'll twist your head off your neck.'

'Since when, my bullwhacker friend, did you become a champion of womanhood? You, with a squaw on every reservation between Fort Apache, Arizona, and the Flathead. The last man who wanted to wrestle, Fogarty, had his guts ripped open before he got a strangle hold.' Quensel's upper lip lifted like an animal's showing his white teeth.

'Quit it, you two,' growled Pete Kaster. 'This ain't no time to be wranglin' over a female. Let's get down to business.'

'United we stand,' said Quensel. 'Divided we fall. Hang together or we might hang separately. Kaster's right. I'll pass the word that the Stranglers will meet at midnight at Fogarty's warehouse.'

The gambler's hand came from beneath his coat where he carried a pearl handled dagger. He was faster with that weapon than most men were with a gun. He could, with a flip of his hand, hit a card at fifteen paces.

Quensel quit his chair with a smooth, catlike grace and left the room.

CHAPTER THREE

Bryce Bradford smiled grimly at the thought of being trapped here at Buffalo Run, held prisoner until those two men from Utah returned from a fruitless hunt for him across the Canadian border. The Avenging Angels were thorough in their methods. They were more deadly than any Vigilante gun-toters or the hired killers of Buffalo Run. Men stared at him curiously as he walked into the El Dorado. He saw Judge Plato Morgan at the bar reciting some ballad, with Fogarty and Kaster and a group of half drunken men an appreciative audience. Bryce was not certain whether Big Tim Fogarty really enjoyed hearing the recitations or whether he was baiting the white-maned old judge.

Men moved back from the bar to give him a place, but they were not making any friendly overtures that might displease Jack Quensel.

Bryce turned to find the gambler at his elbow. His hand dropped to his gun. Quensel smiled thinly and shook his head.

'I'm not playing Decker's hand out, Bradford,' Quensel said.

The bar-tender shoved a glass and small bottle of mineral water across the bar. Quensel filled his glass. The men who lined the long bar watched, diverting their attention from Plato Morgan to the owner of the El Dorado.

'Welcome to Buffalo Run, Bradford,' said Jack Quensel. He lifted his glass and drank.

The crowd relaxed. Quensel was accepting the stranger who had killed Decker.

But Bryce was not quite sure of the gambler's sincerity. There was something about Quensel's eyes and the faint twist of his mouth that belied this friendly gesture. Bryce wasn't trusting Jack Quensel for a minute.

He was about to turn and leave the saloon when a woman's throaty voice said in his ear, 'I'd like to shake the hand that held the gun that shot Charlie Decker.'

He was vaguely aware of the sudden hush of voices in the saloon. The eyes of the tall slender girl were almost on a level with his. Amber eyes matched the mass of tawny hair and the golden texture of her skin. There was no trace of face powder or rouge on her cheeks or natural scarlet lips. She wore a golden yellow evening gown, low cut to show the swell of firm rounded breasts. Her faint smile put a strange warmth in her eyes that were shadowed by soot-black fringed eyelashes.

She was by far the most exotically beautiful woman that Bryce had ever looked at. He felt the dull red flush of embarrassment as he tried to look away.

'Women aren't allowed at the bar,' she said, linking her bare arm through his with a meaning pressure. 'The stage show is just starting, we'll watch it together from my box.' Her eyes met Quensel's and slid away. Her throaty laugh had a challenge in it.

Bryce was painfully aware of the hard stares of every man lined up at the bar as she led him away. His feet felt awkward in mud caked boots. He could feel the brush of the girl's long thigh against his.

Her free hand shoved aside the dark red drapes as she ushered him into the last box. Bryce pulled aside the curtain at the front of the box and saw the stage and entire floor below. Then he let the curtain drop.

When he turned around, the girl twisted against him and her lips fastened on his and held with a bruising force. He felt the hard thrust of her breasts as her slim length moved with a sensuous slowness that quickened his pulse. The blood pounded in his throat and temples. His senses reeled. Never before had he felt anything like this intoxication. The musky odor of her hair and body cloyed in his nostrils as the girl clung to him with a primitive, savage fervor.

Bryce was dizzy headed, taut and quivering inside with strange aroused emotions, when her hands pushed him away with provocative slowness. Her pale eyes were filmed over with a thin glaze under lowered eyelids. Her wide red lips were curled back from strong white teeth. Her quick breath was hot, feverish against his face as she pushed him into one of the chairs. Then she straightened up with an unsteady shaky laugh.

Bryce sat tensely in his chair as she twisted the cork of a champagne bottle in a bucket of chopped ice. When the cork popped she filled two glasses and handed one to Bryce.

There was a strange unreality about the whole thing, like a mixed-up dream. The nearness of the beautiful girl, the lithe movements of her sensuous body, the musk of her tawny hair, the husky voice. All of it had a strange power that left him helpless, and because there was an element of danger it added spice to his desire for her.

There was a faint smile on her lips as she stood just beyond his reach.

'It's my job, Bryce Bradford,' she said in a voice vibrant with emotion, 'to soften you up. Get you drunk enough on wine and kisses to loosen your tongue. I'm to find out who Bryce Bradford is. Where he came from. What brings him to Buffalo Run.'

'Why?' Bryce asked, the words harsh in his tight throat.

'Strangers who are fast with a gun are not welcome here. Your number is up, Bryce.' She reached for the wine bottle and filled her glass and drank slowly.

'Why are you telling me all this?' Bryce asked.

'Since I can remember I've had to fight for an existence. I was tossed with a child's body into a man's world. I learned to fight with a man's weapons and a woman's treachery and deceit. I made my body into a beautiful weapon and used it in my hatred for all men.' Her laugh had an ugly sound as she leaned across the table.

'Here at Buffalo Run I'm known as Quensel's woman. But Nile belongs to no man on earth.' There was a strange mixture of provocative mockery in her smile. She bent over and pulled up the hem of her skirt to show a webbed black silk stocking such as worn by can-can dancers, encasing a beautiful slender leg. There was the smooth ivory length of shapely thigh showing. From a yellow silk garter that held the high stocking in place she took a long thin blade with a pearl handle from the sheath.

'I was going to kill Charlie Decker with this tonight,' she held the knife palmed in her hand, then twisted the blade to catch the lamplight. 'You saved me that trouble when you shot him.' Her lips twisted in a smile that held no warmth. 'Decker used narcotics. One night when he was snowed under I got him to make out and sign a paper that gave me his half-interest in the El Dorado if he should die or get killed. I have the paper safely hidden. Last night Decker tried to get it back with a threat. He pushed me around and I knew he'd kill me if I didn't kill him first.'

She leaned across the table, lowering her voice. 'How would you like to own Jack Quensel's half-interest in the El Dorado? Be my partner in the business?' she asked.

Bryce shook his head, puzzled, the

forced grin on his face twisted out of shape.

'I'm a cowpuncher, lady. Not a gambler or saloon man,' he said.

'I'll handle the gambling and the rest of it,' Nile told him. 'I need a man I can trust all the way down the line.'

'You mean a killer?' Bryce said bluntly.

'If it becomes necessary, yes.'

'You better get another man. Gunslingers hire out cheap.'

'I want a man named Bryce Bradford. And I usually get what I go after.'

'You don't mean this man, lady. I'm drifting directly Plato Morgan gets things shaped around to the law and order he wants.'

The thin stem of the wine glass snapped in her fingers. The wine spilled across the table. The glass rolled off and smashed on the floor. Her short laugh was as brittle as the shattered glass.

'Quensel will cut Morgan into the discard when he's out-lived his purpose. His big mouth has declared his own death warrant. And yours. Tomorrow or next week or next month, whenever the time is right Judge Plato Morgan will be dead. Murdered, to put it bluntly. And if you choose to accept that tin badge, you too will be dead. And that will leave Buffalo Run without a man to protect Virginia Morgan against Jack Quensel who aims to get her, even if he has to marry her.

'I know this mudhole of Buffalo Run and every man who hangs out here. Jack Quensel owns the town and runs every damn man who jumps around when he cracks the whip.' Her hand reached out and closed tight over his. 'A pack of mongrels trained to lay down and roll over, sit up and beg for drinks.'

The heavy red drapes at the entrance of the box moved agitatedly. Bryce's gun was in his hand, his thumb on the hammer when a waiter called out.

'Miss Nile! They're hollerin' for Bryce Bradford downstairs!'

'If that drunken mob wants him, let them come after him,' Nile told the waiter.

'You got it all wrong, Miss Nile. They just voted Bryce Bradford into the sheriff's office and Plato Morgan in as judge. Every man in town has voted them in. Quensel said for me to come up with the news.'

'Tell Quensel that Bryce Bradford got his message,' Nile said.

When the waiter had gone the girl looked at Bryce, her eyes clouded with suspicion.

'Quensel has checked the bet to you, Bryce. But don't forget to remember he has the deal. Every card is marked. Think it over before you buy chips in their game.'

Bryce nodded and shoved his gun back into its holster. 'Looks like it's up to me to play my hand out, regardless,' he said grimly.

'It's on account of Plato Morgan,' Nile said tonelessly as her eyes met his. 'On account of his daughter, the virgin of Buffalo Run.' Her upper lip curled back.

'I reckon that's about the size of it, Nile,' Bryce forced a grin.

'I'm glad you didn't try to lie out of it, Bryce.'

'I'm a hell of a poor liar,' he kept grinning.

'And I'd be lying behind my teeth if I told you I wished you luck with Virginia Morgan.'

Bryce shook his head. 'I told you before that I'm drifting. When I leave Buffalo Run I'm traveling alone.'

'What are you running away from?' The question came abruptly.

'Trouble,' Bryce admitted. 'Gun trouble. Whenever it catches up with me I got to face it alone.' He looked at her gravely. 'There is no place in my life for a woman.

That's hard for you to understand, because you're a woman.' Bryce's words sounded inadequate in his own ears.

'On the contrary, Bryce. I know what you're talking about. And I know what you're up against here in Buffalo Run far better than you do, mister man.' Her eyes were cold, calculating.

'I'll lay it on the line. The girl who got you into this dangerous fix couldn't get you out of the mess even if she knew how.' Her lips curled contemptuously. 'You need a diagram, Bryce?'

'No.'

'When are you going to quit running and make a stand, Bryce?'

'Hard to tell, Nile.'

'Buffalo Run could be as good a place as any.' Her eyes held his.

'I was thinking the same thing,' Bryce said. 'The way things are shaping up I'm caught in the broad middle.'

'That's about the size of it, if you're fool enough to let Quensel pin a phony tin law badge on your shirt.' She reached out and gripped his hand. 'I don't know who's on your trail or why, but I can arrange it for your quick getaway between now and daybreak. You can travel alone or take me with you. I can ride and I can take my own part.

I know a hideout where we can hole up and nobody can get to us without being shot down.'

Nile was standing close to him now. There was a strange look in her eyes. A reckless, dangerous glint that backed up her every word. There was a set to the line of her wide mouth and she was breathing fast.

Bryce had heard tell of women who led an outlaw life and shared whatever dangers and hardships there were to endure without complaint. Content with a few reckless hours of pleasure that balanced the scales. This girl was offering to share his hunted life, without questioning the why or wherefore or the cause behind it.

No man worthy of the name could discount or ignore the sheer magnetism of her nearness. Somehow Bryce knew that Nile was offering him something that she had never before offered to any man. Her closeness was as heady as strong wine and far more potent and lasting.

Bryce's every nerve was pulled tight as a keyed-up fiddle string as they stood close to each other. Split seconds became eternity, time lost value as they stood close without touching.

Then from below on the stage came the

tipsy voice of Judge Plato Morgan. In a maudlin voice he shouted, 'The men who have held this election are clamouring for the presence of Bryce Bradford! Release yourself, Sheriff, from the sinful embrace of that jezebel. Descend and take a man's place among men! Accept the high honour the citizens of Buffalo Run have bestowed upon you!'

Angered beyond all reason Bryce pulled the front curtains apart. His hard cold stare flicked the white-maned judge as he stood in the center of the stage, his handsome face flushed with liquor and the excitement within him. Then Bryce saw Big Tim Fogarty and Pete Kaster standing together, a little apart from the milling drunken crowd. Jack Quensel stood alone at the far end of the bar, a tall glass in his hand. His eyes were fixed on the box above and Bryce felt the triumphant cold enmity of the gambler's pale eyes. A sardonic grin twisted the thin lipped mouth.

Then the swinging half-doors were flung back on their hinges. Virginia Morgan took a quick step inside and stood there for a long moment in the smoke filled lamplight of the El Dorado. She had changed to a somewhat worn and shabby divided skirt made of buckskin, and a silk blouse. Her burnished coppery hair hung down behind her back and her grey eyes were shadowed, her face chalk white. Her tan boots were covered with mud. She held a riding crop gripped in her hand.

When she caught sight of her father, her hurt cry broke across the silence that had fallen over the room at her entrance. She crossed to the stage quickly to stand beside the bewildered man, cold fury and humiliation choking the words in her throat as she trembled in a pent up wrath that could find no outlet.

For once Judge Morgan was at a loss for words. The effects of the whisky quickly soured and died within him as he stood with his daughter in the merciless glare of the footlights, facing a crowd of drunken men and their staring eyes.

'God help us!' The words that came from Virginia Morgan's throat were torn loose from some hidden depth. Then the girl collapsed and lay at her father's feet as motionless as a grey dove shot down by a hunter.

Bryce swung both legs over the edge of the box, hung for a few seconds by his hands then dropped twenty feet to the stage. He had the unconscious girl picked up and in his arms when Nile came down the stairway and motioned him towards the small side door she was holding open.

Bryce moved fast across the stage, the judge at his heels. They followed Nile outside and along a dark alleyway behind the El Dorado, then across a vacant clearing about a hundred yards to a whitewashed log cabin with a white picket fence. Thick morning glory vines climbed wooden trellises on the wide veranda. The yard was planted in flowers of every description. Sweetpea vines grew along the picket fence to make a hedge and the wide plank walk from the gate to the porch was shaded by purple lilac bushes. The windowsills and shutters were painted a soft blue, in contrast to the red brick fireplace chimney. A stone's throw behind the cabin flowed the creek with giant cottonwood trees and thickets of wild rose bushes.

There was a light behind the curtained front windows and as they approached the veranda steps the door opened. A fat squaw in a voluminous calico dress and scrubbed moon face blocked the doorway. The squaw had a formidable look as she stood there, the lamplight behind her and a double-barreled sawed-off shotgun gripped in her hands.

The levered shotgun slowly lowered as

she recognized Nile when she spoke. 'Get the bed ready, Rose. I have brought a sick girl who needs our attention.'

The squaw turned and padded back on moccasined feet, putting the gun on a rack in the hall near the door.

'Rose is my guardian angel,' smiled Nile. 'A shotgun chaperone.'

When Bryce had laid the girl on the bed Nile told him to take Judge Morgan into the front room while she and Rose put Virginia to bed.

Books lined the shelves of the front room that was furnished in heavy polished mahogany. A big silver tip grizzly bear rug was on the floor in front of the fireplace. A spinet piano occupied one corner of the room. The heavy silver and cut glass on the sideboard were in good taste, as were the rest of the furnishings throughout the house.

Judge Morgan poured whisky from a decanter into a whisky glass, and held it in his hand, staring into nothingness. When he spoke it was with contrition and a little sadness.

'I have maligned the reputation of a good woman,' he said, a film of unshed tears in his eyes. 'I've befouled the air with maudlin mouthings in the presence of a motley gathering of drunken companions. A spendthrift of tongue. Let shame lower my head to receive the heaping coals, red from the fires of hell.' The judge mopped the moisture of mingled sweat and tears from his face with a silk handkerchief.

Bryce knew that in spite of his flowery speech, the man was wholly sincere in his self-condemnation.

Nile came into the room. She had changed to a house dress of bleached linen that brought out the golden color of her skin and eyes.

'Your daughter is running a high fever, Mr. Morgan,' she told the judge. 'I have sent an Indian boy to Fort Benton with an urgent note to the doctor. Until he gets here Rose and I will do the best we can.' She looked at the judge with troubled eyes and asked, 'How long has it been since Virginia has had a decent meal?'

A dark flush came into the judge's face. His hands went out in a flat gesture. 'Our credit is no longer good at the store. The larder is bare. Quensel offered to renew our credit but my daughter refused his charity. Would be to God we had never left the State of Virginia,' he spoke fervently, the bitterness of regret in his voice.

Nile forestalled any speech that might be

43

forthcoming by crossing the room with a lithe stride to put a drink in the judge's re-luctant eager hand.

'Drink it down,' she said gently. 'There's times when a man needs a drink. More than he needs absolution for his past sins.'

She poured pale sherry from the other decanter into a glass for herself. She quirked an eyebrow at Bryce. 'That goes for you, too,' she said with a smile.

Bryce poured about two fingers of whisky into a glass and held it until Nile lifted her glass and said, 'Let me be the first to congratulate both of you when you take your oath of office.'

Bryce saw the challenge in her eyes. It was both a challenge and a promise of her support and something else beyond his comprehension. With it came a strange clarity of thought and final decision. It showed in his eyes and every line that etched his face as he drank.

Judge Morgan's futile words were choked down with the emotion that rendered him voiceless.

Nile took him by the arm and led him to the bedroom where his daughter lay propped up on pillows drinking the strong beef broth Rose was feeding her.

A dozen wax candles in a tall heavy silver

candelabra lighted the table with its white linen and polished silver and cut glass as they sat down to dinner.

The judge carved the roast beef. Mashed potatoes, sourdough biscuits, corn on the cob and greens fresh from the garden were on the table. Home-made butter and thick cream and strong black coffee, with strawberry shortcake for dessert.

It was the finest meal Bryce Bradford had ever sat down to and he said so. It was an hour until midnight by the high old-fashioned clock that chimed the half-hour and hour. Nile was a gracious hostess in every way.

No mention was made of the danger that the hour of midnight might bring. The table conversation had the tang of the wine that was served with the meal. The judge's anecdotes matched Nile's gay banter. Even Bryce had shaken off the burden of dread. There was a recklessness to his grin and it showed in the glint of his eyes.

When the hands of the big clock pointed a quarter of an hour before midnight it was time for the men to depart.

The judge tiptoed into the bedroom to take a last look at his daughter. Nile and Bryce were in the shadowed way in an awkward silence as they stood apart like strangers. Then Bryce reached out and pulled her into his arms and their lips met and clung for a long time.

When they heard Judge Morgan coming they pulled apart. Bryce took his cartridge belt and holstered six-shooter from the hall rack. The judge's voice choked with emotion as he gripped Nile's hand and thanked her warmly for all she had done.

When they were outside the white picket gate and plodding across the moonlit stretch of drying ground, Bryce halted, his hand on his gun. He had caught sight of two horsebackers skylighted on the high bluff that gave the town of Buffalo its name. There was something familiar about the pair of night riders, the way they sat their horses as they rode the skyline. As remembrance came, his lips spread in a flat grin. The hard, brooding look came back into his eyes as his grip on his gun tightened.

They were the Avenging Angels who had been hounding his trail north, from the badlands of Bryce Canyon in Utah. As he watched them out of sight a cold chill wired down his spine. He stood for a minute in mud that was ankle deep before he took his hand from his gun.

'What's wrong?' The judge spoke in a whisper.

Bryce shrugged off the dread fear and shoved the Colt back into its holster. 'Some horsebackers rode across my grave,' he said with a forced grin as he walked on towards the lights of Buffalo Run ahead of the older man.

A crowd of men lined the plank walks. As the hour of midnight approached they had come out from the dozen saloons to await the coming of Judge Morgan and Bryce Bradford.

The El Dorado was in total darkness. Quensel had closed the saloon until after the funeral of Charlie Decker.

Bryce sensed the tension that held the men gripped in a grim hand as he and the judge walked down the middle of the street toward Tim Fogarty's warehouse at the end of town as the midnight hour approached.

Those same men who had so readily shouted their unanimous vote for Judge Morgan and Bryce Bradford, had been outwitted, outmaneuvered. Even as they toasted an overwhelming victory in crowded bars, the Stranglers, bound by secret oath, had, one by one, come into the warehouse by way of a back door. Now they were barricaded behind locked doors and shuttered windows, heavily armed and masked.

It was only when the two men neared the warehouse door that they found their way blocked by the crowd that now milled the street. Bryce recognized old Dad Jones, the barnman.

'Tell it to the Judge, Dad, lay it on the line like we told you!' came a voice from the crowd.

'The boys got it figured,' Dad Jones blurted out the words, 'that you two might be bulldozed into takin' the Stranglers' oath, once you get inside and the doors locked. There's some got the notion it was a put up job from the start. They think you are in cahoots with the big three.' The grizzled barnman's eyes narrowed. 'There's twenty-five Stranglers inside and we had it made to set fire to the buildin' and smoke 'em out. We was just waitin' till you showed up.'

'Violence begets violence,' Judge Morgan said with sober dignity. 'In the name of law and order I ask that you men disperse.'

Bryce took a step forward and the crowd that blocked the doorway backed away. Then the door of the warehouse opened and the two men walked inside. The wooden bar made an audible rasping sound as it locked the door behind them.

A raised platform about six-feet square made a raw scraping noise as it was pushed from a corner into the center of the room by a couple of masked men. A long rope with a hangman's knot was lowered slowly from the ridge log of the high beamed ceiling until the noose hung limply a few feet above the platform.

'Are you ready to take the oath of office of judge, Morgan?' Quensel asked from the shadows.

'I came prepared to take that oath,' came the firm reply, 'but not under the intimidation of such trappings. Masked men and a hangman's rope.'

A tall man with a black silk handkerchief covering the lower part of his face came into the yellow glow of the overhead lamp. He carried a large black leather bound Bible in both hands.

Quensel ignored Judge Morgan's remark. He told the masked man to swear the judge into office. When the words of the solemn oath had been repeated by Plato Morgan, Quensel called Bryce Bradford to the platform.

'Are you ready and willing to be sworn in as sheriff?' Quensel asked Bryce.

'I'm ready,' Bryce answered, his eyes fixed on the gambler's.

Even as Bryce Bradford repeated the oath he felt the trap closing in on him. It was like the cold clammy hand of death as he watched the noose with the knot hanging limp and empty and ready. It was only a matter of time until it would be fitted around his neck.

By some trick of lighting the shadow of the rope hung between Quensel and Bryce Bradford. It fell across the Bible like a wide black ribbon, a sinister marker, as Bryce slowly repeated the final words of his oath of office.

A loud pounding on the door interrupted the proceedings. Every man's hand dropped to his gun.

The guard at the door was told to see who it was.

The mud-smeared man who staggered in, cursing thickly, was Jerry O'Toole, Tim Fogarty's stagedriver.

'I was set afoot fifteen miles back on Cottonwood Creek,' he told Fogarty who had asked him what had happened. 'I hoofed it in. The hold-up gent made me unhook the horses and turn 'em loose. He killed the shotgun guard and shot the lock off the strong-box. He sent me on my way with Winchester bullets singing around me like hornets.'

Big Tim Fogarty looked at Quensel. 'The stage was held up. What do you make of it, Quensel?' he said.

'I'd say,' said the gambler, his voice sharp, 'that the new sheriff has his first job cut out for him. He can pick his posse from these Stranglers and take the trail before it gets cold. I was expecting sixty-thousand dollars in currency in that strong-box from the Fort Benton Bank.'

'I don't need a posse,' Bryce spoke up quickly. 'How many hold-up men were there?' he turned and asked the stagedriver.

'I saw only one man but there might have been another feller hid out in the thick brush. When the hold-up feller told the shotgun guard to lift his hands, I kicked my brake on and quit my seat and lay in the mud playin' possum. I'm drawin' stagedrivers's pay and don't get paid to referee a gun fight.

'When the Wells Fargo shotgun messenger falls over dead, a tall feller in a yellow slicker with a black handkerchief across his face kicked me in the ribs and told me to unhook the four horses and pull the harness off. Then he told me to start walking for Buffalo Run and not to look back. "Lot's wife," he said, "looked back and was turned into a pillar of salt. I'll turn you into something just as dead if you don't keep movin'." '

'What did he look like?' Bryce asked. 'The one you saw.'

'He'd stand six feet and he was neither skinny nor porky. He moved quick and talks as quiet as if he was passin' the time of day.'

'I'll need a good horse,' Bryce turned to Fogarty.

'You don't know the country,' said Big Tim. 'Better take a posse.'

'The ground should be soft enough for trackin'. There's only one hold-up man for sure. A posse would get in one another's way.'

CHAPTER FOUR

Bryce Bradford shoved past Quensel and Fogarty and Kaster who were close grouped around the luckless stagedriver. He slid the heavy bar back and pulled the door open, motioning to the judge to follow him.

The crowd of men who still filled the street were eyeing Bryce and the judge uncertainly. Curiosity mingled with suspicion was written in their eyes and their wordless questioning.

Old Dad Jones limped forward, his eyes cold and bright. 'How'd you make out?' he asked.

'I'm the Sheriff of Buffalo Run,' Bryce grinned twistedly, 'if that means anything. Plato Morgan has taken his oath as judge.'

The grizzled barnman jerked a thumb towards the building. 'How about the Stranglers? Them sonsabitches still run the town?'

'Judge Morgan will fetch you up to date, Dad. The stage has been held up. I'm going out after the road-agents. I'll need a stout grain fed horse.'

'I can still handle a gun and travel the

route, Bryce,' Old Dad said.

Bryce grinned faintly and shook his head. 'I'm going alone, Dad.'

Old Dad snorted. He opened his mouth to say something, then changed his mind. 'Come along, Sheriff,' he said. 'I'll mount you on the best damned hoss you ever throwed a leg over.' He shoved through the crowd. 'Open up a lane for the Sheriff of Buffalo Run,' he said waspishly.

When they were beyond earshot, he said, 'You're a damned fool, boy. High time somebody told you what you're up against. Hell's fire! Them road-agents is in cahoots with Quensel. They're hired hands drawin' down fightin' pay. Fogarty owns the stage line and works in with Quensel and Pete Kaster, Decker when he was alive.

'When I stake you to this ridge-runner, Bryce, you drift and keep on going till you're plumb outa the country. Don't try to pick up the trail of those road-agents or you'll run slap-dab into the bushwhacker trap they got set for you.'

Dad led the way into the lantern light of the barn. He limped down between the rows of stalls. 'Gawdamighty, they're gone!' Dad Jones fouled the air with profanity. 'Either some hoss thief got away with them or those two Square and Compass killers came back.'

Bryce grinned mirthlessly as he walked on. He went into a stall that held a big brown gelding wearing Pete Kaster's brand. He led the horse out.

'That's Pete Kaster's private,' Dad told him. 'Best damn hoss in the barn. Pete will blow up like a powder keg.'

'Let his friends pick up the chunks.' Bryce saddled the big brown. He shoved his Winchester carbine into its saddle scabbard and mounted. 'Take good care of my horse till I get back, Dad,' he said as he rode away.

He tied the horse to the hitchrack in front of Nile's log cabin. He crossed the porch and rapped on the door. When nobody came he opened it and walked in. There was nobody at home except Virginia Morgan who called, 'Come in, please,' from the bedroom.

Bryce walked into the bedroom. Virginia was still in bed, propped up by pillows. She said the doctor had come from Fort Benton and he'd told her to stay in bed until she regained her strength from malnutrition. She said Nile had gone out on an errand and that Rose had gone home for the day.

'I'm glad you came, Bryce,' she said,

forcing a wan smile. 'I wanted to see and talk to you. Please sit down. I want to talk to you about my father. Where is he? Is he all right? I mean. . . .' Her hands clenched into tight fists. 'Are those men making a fool of him again?' Her eyes were darkened with worry, her lower lip clenched between small white teeth.

'The judge was cold sober,' Bryce sat down in the chair beside the bed. 'He'll be along directly. He was just sworn into office.'

'Then he wasn't lying. It wasn't just an excuse to get back to the El Dorado. I didn't believe him because he has been tricked so many times by those men with promises.'

Her head lifted proudly. 'Don't misunderstand me. My father is the finest man on earth. He was a Major in the Confederate Army, on General Robert E. Lee's private staff. After Lee's surrender and he came home, it was a terrible blow to find his plantation gone, his wife dead and his daughter living on the charity of friends in Richmond.' Her chin quivered as she fought back the tears.

'I didn't mean to pour out our troubles to a stranger,' she said. 'But I have to get my father out of this town. He has a few friends at Fort Benton and can go into law practice with a boyhood friend there. He lost all our money at poker here and was too proud, too ashamed to reach Fort Benton penniless. Decker and Quensel both offered us help, but there were conditions.'

Bryce took her small delicate hand in his and told her she had nothing more to worry about. He reached inside his shirt and unbuckled the money belt he wore around his waist, and tossed it on the bed.

'I came to give this to the judge before I left town. There's five thousand dollars in it. It's all yours. I may not come back alive.'

Virginia looked at him, bewilderment in her eyes. Then she shoved the money belt away like it was a snake that had crawled up on her bed.

'Take it easy lady,' Bryce shoved back his chair. 'My horse is saddled. I'm pulling out in a few minutes. Chances are I'll never get back to Buffalo Run. There's no strings to that money. Your father has befriended me and I want him to have this money,' Bryce backed towards the door.

'You've no reason to treat me nice,' Virginia told him. 'I haven't even thanked you for all you've done. But before you leave I want you to know that I think you're a good man, Bryce Bradford. Take care of yourself in this town or they'll kill you,' she warned.

'I'll see what I can do to get your father to take you away from Buffalo Run,' Bryce promised her. He hung the money belt over the chair back. 'You need this money worse than I do. Use it,' he said, then left the house.

Quensel and Fogarty and Kaster were waiting for him when he rode into the alley.

'That's my private horse you got saddled,' Pete Kaster snarled.

'That road-agent has a two hour head start,' Big Tim Fogarty complained. 'Maybe this new sheriff is in cahoots with the hold-up man,' he suggested to his two companions.

'Now that the brave lone-handed hero has kissed the gals a fond farewell,' Quensel leered, his hand inside his coat where he packed his knife, 'he's ready to pick up the cold trail. That road-agent got away with sixty thousand dollars of mine. Bring it and the road-agent back, Bradford. Or don't come back!'

Bryce had dismounted and was standing on spread legs, rolling a cigarette while his hot blooded temper had a chance to simmer down.

'Are you three jaspers talkin' to throw a scare into me?' Bryce asked. 'Or are you trying to prove something to one another?'

Bryce lit his cigarette. He thumbed the burning match into Quensel's eyes. As the gambler brushed the burning stick away, Bryce took a quick step. His hard fist sank into Quensel's belly, just under the lower ribs where the nerve centered in his solar plexus. It had all Bryce's hundred and eighty-five pounds behind it.

Quensel's knees buckled, his arms dropped as his eyes rolled back. Bryce slammed a vicious left hook under his lean jaw as the gambler went down to lie motionless on his back in a mud puddle.

The pistol in Bryce's hand moved in a short flat arc to cover the other two men.

'Any further orders you want to give the sheriff?' he asked.

'Only this,' Big Tim Fogarty said, his voice a husky whisper. 'You better finish the job on Quensel. That's advice, not an order.'

'Pick the knife-slinger up and bed him down beside his dead partner,' Bryce told them. 'When he comes alive give him a message. Tell him that if he ever lays a hand on Nile or Virginia Morgan I'll shove his tinhorn neck in that Stranglers' noose you had made up for me.'

Quensel moaned in agony as his legs doubled up. He rolled over on his side and commenced vomiting.

Bryce saw the folded piece of paper that had dropped from Quensel's pocket as he turned. As he picked it up, he saw Fogarty and Kaster exchange swift sidelong looks. Both pair of eyes had the same panic in them.

'That letter you picked up,' Pete Kaster said harshly, 'belongs to Quensel. Dropped out of his pocket. Hand it over.'

'Hell,' Big Tim Fogarty forced a chuckle. 'It's from one of his women, one of them mushy love letters. Put it back in his pocket, Bradford.'

'I'll give it to him, personally,' Bryce eyed the pair narrowly, 'when I get back.' He put the folded paper carefully into his shirt pocket.

'What gave you the notion you was comin' back?' Pete Kaster bared his stained, discolored teeth in a snarl.

'Shut up, Pete,' Fogarty growled. 'Let's get Quensel back to the El Dorado before he pukes his guts out.'

'Send my horse back or I'll have you

hung for a horse thief,' Kaster said as they picked Quensel up out of the mud puddle.

But Bryce had already ridden off into the night. He was headed for the high bluff where he had seen the pair of Avenging Angels. Long before the coming of the white man the Indians had used the cliff to spook herds of buffalo into stampeding, charging blindly over the fifty foot drop to pile up dead at the base. Then the squaws would gather and butcher the animals and hang the meat in strips to dry. There would be meat for the coming winter and tanned hides for robes and tepee coverings. The high bluffs were called buffalo runs.

Bryce picked up the tracks of two horses and followed them cautiously, leaning sideways from his saddle. As he rode at a running walk he tried to think things out, but thoughts of Virginia Morgan and Nile kept crowding in, and he finally gave it up as a bad job. He'd better keep his senses alert for a bushwhacker gun trap.

First things come first, he told himself. Before he cut sign for the road-agent, he wanted a showdown with the two Avenging Angels. The horse tracks angled towards the wagon road, the same road, rutted deep by freight wagons, that was used by the stage. A crimson-streaked dawn showed on the skyline. When the light was sufficient Bryce took the folded sheet of paper from his pocket and read it. It was the unfinished letter the range detective had written before he was killed by Decker.

This was all the death warrant Bryce needed for Quensel and Fogarty and Kaster. He'd heard that Decker had killed a man named Henry Black the night before he got shot himself.

Bryce had all but convinced himself to turn back to town and have Judge Morgan issue bench warrants for the three men, but changed his mind when he came upon the stagecoach hub deep in mud where the stage road crossed a boggy creek. Horse collars and bridles and harness lay in the mud, the shotgun guard lay face down in an awkward sprawl, one leg twisted under the other, a gun still gripped in his lifeless hand. Drying blood from his bullet-torn body made a sticky red puddle under him. The lid of the strong-box was open. Horse tracks and the tracks of men's boots were all around.

Bryce rode in a slow circle around the empty, deserted coach, his Winchester carbine in the crook of his elbow, reading meaning in the sign.

The locked canvas mail sacks were intact in the leather boot under the driver's seat. The express strong-box only had been looted. Leaning down from his saddle, Bryce peered into the empty strong-box at a piece of white cardboard with crudely printed words on it.

He leaned over and picked the cardboard up. His eyes narrowed as he read the road-agent's cryptic message:

NOTICE AND WARNING! TO WHOM IT CONCERNS! TITHE HAS BEEN COLLECTED BY THE AVENGING ANGELS. 7 & 11.

The cabalistic numbers that served as a signature had a significance to Bryce Bradford. Every Avenging Angel had his own number. A written name could be held as damning evidence in a court of law, while numbers had no value as evidence, proving no identity to anyone save to those initiated into the secret order.

There was something grim and sinister here that puzzled Bryce. He wondered how and in what way, shape or form Quensel and his dead partner were tied in with the exiled, outcast Mormons who dwelt in the hidden settlement of Rainbow's End in the broken badlands of Bryce Canyon in Utah.

Time had been when the Avenging Angels under the leadership of the giant statured, curly maned and bearded Porter Rockwell, had been the far reaching arm of the law laid down by the Book of Mormon, when the Mormons of Utah were under the stern rule of Apostle Joseph Smith. Those were the blood-spattered final years of lawfully practiced polygamy. The years when Rockwell organized a band of men to mete out punishment to those who disobeyed Mormon law.

The Mountain Meadow massacre of men, women and children by the Mormons brought the United States Army into Utah. The abandonment of the secret killers of the church was ordered, together with the practice of polygamy.

The foolhardy stubborn few Mormons who chose to defy the United States Government were forced into exile, both by our Government and by the Mormon Church.

Those few who fled with their plural wives and children, travelled by wagon train, herding their livestock, migrating to the all but inaccessible, broken-timbered country of Bryce Canyon on the north side of the Colorado river. Their settlement of

Rainbow's End looked down on the vast eternal beauty of the Grand Canyon of the Colorado.

A handful of people. Brave men and women who dared defy the mighty government of the United States in the practice of their belief as written in the Book of Mormon, pointing out that any man was free to practice his own religion without prosecution.

Rainbow's End became the last stand of the outcast Mormons who had been driven from their homeland. There they practiced their religion and their Avenging Angels took care of those who broke the laws.

Bryce Bradford's grandfather had been one of those exiles. An Apostle with only one wife, but nevertheless in sympathy with the self-exiled people. He had led the bitter trek to Bryce Canyon. He had been one of the founders of the forbidden settlement of Rainbow's End. When he and his wife died they left behind one son, Bryce's father, Robert Bradford, who had a streak of rebel in him. When he was chosen to take the secret oath of the Avenging Angels, he revolted.

Robert Bradford had taken his young wife and son and left the forbidden land in the night. He had taken with him only what belonged to him, his horses, his wife and five-year-old son who had been born in the log cabin overlooking the Grand Canyon of the Colorado.

He had broken one of the cardinal laws of Rainbow's End when he left. Because it had been decreed from the beginning that once a man or woman chose to live within the boundaries of the settlement, there they must dwell until they died.

A child born within the forbidden land was governed by the same rule that held the parents confined within its boundaries. Therefore, Bryce Bradford came under the laws of the outcasts and within the far reach of the long riders who enforced the laws.

Bryce had always been aware of the futility of escape. Sooner or later those long riders would close the gap. If he showed fight now, those two Avenging Angels were bound by oath to shoot him down. If he surrendered, he would be taken back to Rainbow's End to stand trial before the Apostles of the Latter Day Saints as written in the Book of Mormon.

Since the exiles of Rainbow's End were guided by the Book of Mormon, they were duty bound to pay tithe to the Mormon Church at Salt Lake City in Utah.

Surely the gambler Quensel had no connection with the outcast Mormons, nor with the Mormon Church. No man abiding by the strict laws set down by the Book of Mormon was ever the owner of a saloon or gambling house. Both Quensel and his dead partner were far, far below the level of the moral standard of living of a decent Mormon, even those who drank and gambled and committed adultery, known derisively as Jack-Mormons.

Bryce scrutinized the wording of the message that puzzled him, for the last time. Then he leaned from his saddle and replaced the cardboard.

It was up to him now to pick up the trail left by the two Avenging Angels. He was remembering what Jerry O'Toole had quoted the hold-up man as saying, 'Lot's wife looked back and was turned into a pillar of salt.' The two killers from Rainbow's End would be able to quote from the Bible.

Their trail was plain for Bryce Bradford to find and follow. Bryce stiffened at the thought. Those two men had a motive in setting the stagedriver afoot. They had been in Buffalo Run and knew that a stranger named Bryce Bradford had just been elected sheriff. They had gotten their horses out of the barn and ridden back to the stagecoach to leave the cryptic message and a plain trail for him to follow.

Bryce had a strong hunch where they were headed for.

CHAPTER FIVE

Jack Quensel gritted back a low moan of agony and opened his eyes. They had laid him beside Decker's open coffin. He rolled away from the black box and swung his legs to the floor. He was bent over a little as he took a couple of steps and dropped his sick weight into a chair. His sleek hair hung down in dank strands across his pale sweat beaded forehead.

'Sheriff Bryce Bradford,' Big Tim Fogarty mused aloud. 'When he hits a man, by hell, he stays hit. Like bein' kicked by an army mule, eh Quensel?' A grin spread his whiskered face but his eyes were cold.

Quensel lifted his head. 'What the hell were you sorry yellow bastards doing while he worked me over?'

'Lookin' into the round, black hole of his gun barrel,' Big Tim chuckled. 'I told you you'd got a bear by the tail, Quensel.'

'Fetch a pail of water, some towels and a bottle of whisky,' Quensel told them as he shrugged out of his coat.

'Why in hell didn't you burn that letter

69

you took off Decker?' Big Tim growled. 'That new sheriff picked it up when it fell out of your pocket and rode away with it.'

'Why didn't you shoot him?' Quensel's voice was shrill. 'There were two of you.'

'Any time that Bradford feller pulls a gun,' Fogarty said, 'he figures on usin' it.'

'You had your hand on your knife when he hit you in the guts', Pete Kaster sneered. 'He had a gun in his other hand before you knew what hit you.'

Quensel slid from his chair, a deadly short-barrelled derringer in his hand. His thin lips twisted.

'While Charlie Decker was alive,' Quensel said, 'I paid him to do my killing. He was a natural killer who enjoyed his work. His death left me short-handed, and until I hire another killer to take Decker's place, I'll do my own gun chores.

'You two drunken bastards both know where you stand. The El Dorado holds heavy mortgages on the Diamond F freight outfit and stage line. The El Dorado holds controlling interest in Pete Kaster's mining claims and his K cow outfit. Any argument to the contrary?'

'You got us by the short hairs,' Big Tim shrugged massive shoulders. 'No doubt about it, Quensel.'

70

Quensel eyed both men coldly as he held the gun on them.

'The easiest way to foreclose those mortgages is with this gun. Can either of you give me one reason why I shouldn't gut shoot both of you before you do any more talking out of turn?'

Quensel had been fist whipped and these two men had witnessed the humiliation of Bryce Bradford's easy victory. It rankled like poison inside his bruised belly. Both men read murder in the gambler's eyes.

'Off-hand,' Fogarty grinned and shook his head, 'I can't think up a reason.' He chuckled. 'As the saying goes, if I was to die for it.'

There was a heavy pounding on the door, then Jerry O'Toole's whisky voice was saying he'd just brought in the stagecoach and harness. The horses had come in by themselves.

'Did you see anything of the new sheriff?' Quensel asked.

'Nary a sign. But I found this message inside the strongbox. It makes no sense to me.' He read the message aloud before he handed the piece of cardboard to Quensel.

The blood had drained from the gambler's face, leaving it grey as death. The hand that gripped the snub-nosed gun was white-knuckled. 'What the hell,' Big Tim Fogarty's voice was heavy with suspicion and puzzlement, 'is a tithe?'

'A tithe,' volunteered Pete Kaster, 'is a Mormon tax assessment. Every Mormon pays his yearly tithe from his earnings to the Mormon Church. If he don't pay tithe, they send their Avenging Angels out to collect.'

'What the hell has a tithe tax got to do with holding up one of my stagecoaches?' asked Fogarty. 'I ain't no Mormon.'

'Old Dad Jones told me,' Jerry O'Toole spoke up, 'that those two Square and Compass geldings he had in the barn are gone. Two fellers came and got them during all the big election excitement. They left the two horses Fogarty sold them in the feed yard. That Square and Compass horse brand is used by the Avenging Angels of the Mormons.'

'Well, I'll be damned!' Fogarty said, puzzling it out. 'Then it was that goat-whiskered gent and his big, overgrown son that held up the stage.'

Quensel had been standing silent, his stare fixed, as if he hadn't heard a single word of what was being said.

'Shut up, all of you,' the gambler cut in like a knife blade. 'Let Jerry out and shut the door, Pete.' The cold threat in Quensel's eyes was backed up by the gun in his hand.

When the stagedriver had gone, Quensel asked, 'Did either of those Square and Compass men talk to you, Tim?'

'The big one with the billy-goat whiskers did the talkin',' Fogarty said. 'But outside of the horse dicker, he didn't say a word that ties in with the hold-up. He never said where they came from or why they were here, just that they had a long ride to make. They paid two weeks' feed bill in advance and said they'd be back for their horses.'

'Wade Applegate whose ranch lies between the Bear Paws and the Little Rockies,' the gambler said, 'comes from the Mormon country in Utah. At one time he was a high ranking Apostle of the Church. I have a hunch those two held up the stage and are headed for Applegate's hidden ranch in the badlands, with sixty thousand dollars of my money. And I suspect our newly elected sheriff is close behind them.' Quensel's thin smile left his eyes cold as he picked up the cardboard and read the grim message.

He too, was remembering what Jerry O'Toole had quoted the hold-up man as saying about Lot's wife. The hold-up man knew his Bible.

'I'm betting,' Fogarty snorted angrily, 'that you know more about this than you're sayin', Quensel. Better lay your cards face up so a man can read 'em.'

Quensel laughed in Fogarty's face. A short laugh, like splinters cracking. He got up and left the room without speaking.

CHAPTER SIX

Jack Quensel was one of that breed of man who should never touch whisky. One drink and he emptied the bottle, and before it was empty there was another ready.

Sober, Quensel was all that a high stake gambler should be. Cold nerved, cautious, deadly, he played his cards close to his belly and when the bets were down, it was Quensel who raked in the chips.

Drunk, Quensel was ugly, swaggering, quarrelsome, treacherous. He killed without a hint of warning, knifed or shot a man in the back.

Whisky warped his brain, twisted his mentality into grotesque, ugly shape. Brave men gave Quensel a wide berth when he was on one of his habitual drunks. Women, even the hardened percentage girls who danced the can-can at his El Dorado, were wont to vanish when Quensel took his first drink. All the veneer and polish of a gentleman of breeding and education dissolved by the alcohol that poisoned his brain cells and fired his unholy lusts.

No man on earth was more bitterly

aware of this than Quensel himself as he sat slumped in a bar-room chair, the half-emptied whisky bottle in his hand, brooding thoughts of the past he had buried crowding his mind.

When Nile came into the room and stood with her back against the door she had closed, the gambler's thin lips twisted. He picked up the cardboard from the table and motioned with his head for Nile to come over. He tipped the bottle to his lips while she read the message.

'You know where those cheerful tidings came from?' he asked.

'Jerry O'Toole brought me up to date,' Nile said.

Quensel smiled thinly as he lifted the bottle again and drank.

'Did you know that Decker signed a paper leaving his half interest in the El Dorado to me?' Nile asked.

Quensel nodded that he knew.

'I'm buying you out at your own price, Quensel. On one condition. That you leave Buffalo Run, quit Montana and never come back.'

'And if I choose not to sell out?' Quensel asked.

Nile's hand slipped into her jacket pocket, her fingers closing around the butt of a .38. 'I came here prepared to kill you,' she said, her voice deadly.

'All I have left,' Quensel spoke quietly, 'from a misspent life is my doubtful reputation as a high stake gambler, and a true gambler plays his hand out. Even if it's a losing hand.' He twisted the bottle in both hands as he held it between his widespread legs, eyeing it sightlessly as he spoke.

The spots of grey at his temples seemed to have spread and Nile noticed the sprinkle of grey in his thick black hair that was uncombed, dishevelled. There were lines etched deeply on the man's face that she had never noticed before. It was as if he had aged overnight.

He lifted his head and looked at her searchingly. Something of the bitter hardness was gone from his eyes as he smiled. 'You are a remarkable woman, Nile. The most beautiful woman I have ever known, with a woman's courage that shames the bravest of men.' The smile faded. His eyes went black.

A slow flush came into her cheeks. She had her lower lip bitten between her teeth. 'Damn you,' she licked a drop of blood from her lip. 'Damn you, Quensel.' Her hand came from her pocket empty, ringless.

'Get out, Nile,' Quensel told her in a dead voice. 'Get away from me, before I cut your beautiful throat.'

Nile backed away from his eyes. She opened the door and went out, closing it on the gambler and his bottle.

Tonight when Jack Quensel had need of all that cold deadly calm gambler's mind, he had reached for the bottle. No man in Buffalo Run knew what had caused Quensel to take his first drink at the bar. No man alive knew. But a woman named Nile Carter knew the reason, even as she knew beforehand that he would get drunk before tomorrow came.

Charlie Decker, if he were alive, would know the cause. Tithe was only part payment on the balance due. Quensel and Decker had been drunk together that Christmas Eve a year ago when they had incurred a debt that would be paid off in full by the Avenging Angels from Rainbow's End.

Decker had gotten a tip-off that there was to be close to seventy-five thousand dollars on the stage they had held up that night. Too big a haul to trust to any hired road-agents or to share with Pete Kaster or Tim Fogarty. The memory of the hold-up came back now with startling clarity, as

Quensel poured a drink and sat with brooding thoughts.

'There's a big fat Christmas cake in the Wells Fargo strong-box,' Decker had needled him. 'Too big a plum cake to cut more than two ways, Quensel.'

There had been four passengers inside the buckled-down canvas curtains of the stagecoach that night. The snow shone like Christmas tree decorations on the scrub pine thicket that had hidden Quensel and Decker in long fur coats and muskrat caps, black silk mufflers across their faces.

Quensel had drunk to drown the memories of other Christmas Eves that came to haunt him as he and Decker had waited. Poignant memories of gay parties and the perfume of a golden-haired girl with his engagement ring on her finger. A past that Quensel never spoke of and had left buried along his back trail.

He was remembering how Jerry O'Toole, the stagedriver, had sleighbells buckled between the hames of his six-horse team. He had shared his jug with the shotgun guard on the seat beside him. Both men a little drunk and singing off-key as the stagecoach rounded the bend, 'Jingle-bells, jingle-bells, jingle all the way. . . .'

A big man in a fur coat had been the first to step out into the snow, a man with a leathery face and drooping iron-grey moustache. Two other men came out, their hands in the air, then a tall girl in a mink coat and cap and fur boots stepped out, lifting her skirt to show a length of shapely leg. She had stood boot deep in the snow, a faint smile on her wide red lips that were the color of the holly berries pinned to her coat. There had been no trace of fear in her amber eyes.

Decker voiced some vulgar remark about the girl. Quensel slapped him, back handed, across the face hidden behind the muffler. Decker saw the glint of the knife in his hand and stepped back beyond reach.

'Get on with the deal, you foul-mouthed sewer rat,' Quensel had told Decker.

For a long moment their eyes had met and locked in a tight, tense grip of hate. Then Decker's eyes had slid away as he made the half turn. The gun in his hand spat a jet of flame, then a second flame spat through the gun smoke that wisped from his gun-barrel. Two of the men standing knee deep in the snowdrift had doubled up, falling slowly.

The tall man had dropped on one knee beside one of the dead men. His hand groped inside the pocket of the dead man's coat and came out holding a gun. Quensel shot him as he thumbed back the gun hammer.

The shotgun guard had thrown down his gun. His hands were high in the air when Quensel shot him. Quensel had told the girl to get back inside the coach.

Jerry O'Toole was sawing on the lines as the horses jack-knifed. When he had got them straightened out and under control, Quensel had stepped out from behind the ambush.

As he walked out into the cold pale moonlight, he had made a sinister figure in his beaver coat, a gun in his hand. He lifted the curtain to let the moonlight penetrate the dark interior of the coach. The shaft of light had caught the girl unawares.

She was bent over, lifting a black leather satchel from the floor on to the seat with her own luggage. She shoved it between a hatbox and a suitcase and was pulling the buffalo lap robe up over the bags when Quensel's low laugh came from behind the muffler across his face.

'Even a gentleman turned blackguard,' he said mockingly, 'never robs a woman's purse nor strips the rings from her fingers.'

'Thank you,' her husky voice was contemptuous.

'But the black satchel you were concealing does not belong to you, lady. Hand it over.'

When he saw the stubby derringer pistol palmed in her hand, the gun cocked and levelled at him with a steady hand, he had said, 'The lady has courage. The gentleman is mistaken.' The black muffler masked a sardonic grin. 'We may never meet again, lady. Would it be too much to beg the sprig of holly you wear? The red of the berries matches your lips.'

Her free hand unpinned the holly and handed it to him. Their eyes met and held for a long moment.

'Shove that tin cake box off,' Decker's voice crackled at the driver in the cold night. 'Drag the wench out. The stage goes off without her.'

Quensel had stiffened. 'Down on the floor, quick,' he whispered. 'Cover up with the lap robes.' He withdrew his head and pulled the curtain in place.

Quensel turned to face the masked Decker, whose gun was pointed at the belly of the stagedriver who was heaving the strong-box off into a snowdrift.

'Get going, driver,' Quensel ordered. He

eyed Decker bleakly. 'The lady goes on to her destination,' he said, his voice deadly.

'You God damn fool,' Decker spat out. 'You're lettin' that wench put a rope around our necks.'

Jerry O'Toole's long buckskin lash popped like a pistol. The horses lunged and the coach rocked and swayed on its way.

When the stage had rolled out of sight, Quensel had told Decker to frisk the three dead men while he filled the canvas sack he had taken from his saddle, with the money in the strong-box.

There was an official brown envelope on top of the taped money. Quensel slit it open with a knife. There was enough moonlight to read the paper inside. 'For the Fort Benton Bank, consigned by Wade Applegate, to be deposited to the account of the Mormon's Church in Utah. Seventy-five thousand dollars.'

Quensel put the paper in his pocket. When Decker came over, Quensel looked up at him questioningly.

'No identification on any of them,' Decker reported. 'No wallets. No money. Two had guns, the older man was un-armed. Looked like he was a prisoner.'

'I gave the unarmed man a chance for

his taw, Decker,' Quensel said. 'He had a gun in his hand when I shot him. Who knows, perhaps I saved the man from hanging.'

He put the last of the money in the sack and pulled the draw-string tight. 'Seventy-five grand here, Decker, to split two ways,' he said. He unscrewed the cap on a flask and proffered it to Decker.

'You know damn well I never touch whisky, Quensel.'

'You'll take a drink now, to bind the deal that seals our lips to secrecy.'

Decker took a swallow and handed back the flask. 'Secrecy, hell,' he had said. 'Jerry O'Toole knows better than to let out so much as a hint, but the only way to shut a woman's mouth is to kill her.'

'Have you ever killed a woman, Decker?'

'Two.' Decker's teeth showed as his lips skinned back. 'The common law wife I'd been living with. The tart I was shacking up with. Both for the same reason. They gossiped too much about the way I was earning the money I was giving them to spend.'

Decker took two capsules of morphine from a small box and swallowed them. 'I was killing men for the reward they brought. I was a bounty hunter and couldn't afford any loose talk. That's why I never drink. I'll settle for a couple of capsules.'

'You're welcome to the dope, Decker. But one thing; if you ever meet that girl and lay a finger on her, I'll rip your belly open.'

Quensel drank from the flask and walked over to where the three dead men lay in the crimson-stained snow. He stared down at each face, memorizing every feature, then walked to his horse.

'You know who Wade Applegate is, Decker?' he asked.

'Hell, yes. He has a horse ranch hidden in the badlands below the Little Rockies. Raises the best horses in Montana.'

'Wade Applegate comes from the Mormon country in Utah. There's a rumor that he was a high-ranking Apostle of the Mormon Church.'

'What difference does it make, Quensel?'

'Seventy-five thousand dollars. He was sending it to the Mormon Church. That's a hell of a lot of horses to sell.'

'Then the Mormons have donated a Christmas present to you and me.' Decker grinned and swung into his saddle. He rode away, leaving Quensel to follow.

Quensel slid the Winchester from the saddle scabbard when he had mounted his horse. He lined the sights to the three hundred yard notch and held the gun on Decker's fur-coated back, with the hammer thumbed back and his finger on the trigger, until Charlie Decker had ridden out of sight.

He told himself he should kill the bounty hunter now, then decided to let it ride for the present.

A cold sweat beaded his forehead under the sweatband of his hat. His hands were unsteady as he lowered the gun and put it back in the scabbard. He rode along with the uncorked flask in his hand, deep in thought, drinking to get the sound of sleighbells from inside his brain.

A few hours later when Quensel came into the bar at the El Dorado, the bartender leaned across the polished mahogany and whispered, 'There's a swell lookin' gal waitin' to see you in your private office. I sent her a bottle of champagne to keep her company till you showed up. Some men are born lucky.'

It was the girl from the stagecoach . . . Her fur coat and cap lay on a chair and she had a half-emptied wineglass in her hand. The black satchel was on the floor beside her chair.

'I'm Nile Carter,' she said with a smile. 'I came here to make a deal with you, Jack Quensel.' She rose from her chair and holding the gambler with her eyes, she adjusted the spray of holly in his lapel.

When Quensel took her in his arms, a movement like the quiver of a trapped animal swept the length of her body. His wide mouth fastened on hers.

'I play for keeps, Quensel,' the whispered words were in his mouth. 'I want a cut of the El Dorado, a half interest.'

'I have a partner, Charlie Decker. He owns a half interest in the El Dorado.' Quensel's voice was unsteady as he held her in his embrace.

'Deal Decker out', her voice cut like a whetted blade as she freed herself with a twist of her body.

Quensel suddenly reached for her again. Her throaty laugh sounded as he breathed hotly against her breasts.

CHAPTER SEVEN

Bryce Bradford pushed the big brown gelding to a long trot. It gave him no little satisfaction to know that he was forking a horse that would put the miles between him and the men who would be cold-trailing him.

Bryce picked up the trail of the two stage robbers and followed it slowly. He was badly handicapped because of his lack of knowledge of the country. So far, the trail led northward and a little to the west of the stage road to Fort Benton.

Then he lost the trail. Lost it in a bewildering maze of horse tracks. The two lone riders had used an old trick to blot out their sign. They had picked up a bunch of wild horses and had drifted for miles with the loose stock. They had been long-sighted enough to pull the shoes off their own horses.

Bryce slowed to a running walk and let the horse follow in the general direction of the unshod horses. He rode for perhaps fifteen minutes before he came to a decision. The moonlight gave him a fair idea of the topography of the country, hills, coulees, long draws, flats, a square tabletopped mesa to the north. Following horse tracks now was a fool's game. The two men knew every trick and twist of the dangerous role they were playing. They'd probably split up ten miles from here and meet again at some hideout.

Bryce knew that the Little Rockies would be their ultimate destination because he was drawing upon his memory, remembering stories his father had told him before he was killed, about a man named Wade Applegate, a Mormon from Utah, who had come to eastern Montana and bought a ranch. He had described the country and shown Bryce a rough map of the exact location of the ranch.

Bryce's father had described Wade Applegate as being a just and stern man, slow to anger, never making a decisive move until he was absolutely certain he was in the right. A man past his prime of life who had married a full-blood Indian woman in Montana.

Applegate stood for justice towards all men. The two lone riders would find refuge at his ranch, even as the son of Bob Bradford would be welcome and safe under the same roof.

Bryce asked for nothing better than to

meet the two Avenging Angels under the roof of Wade Applegate. Fate seemed to be shaping his destiny, pointing the trail out for him. He had been travelling north and west, now he swung eastward, taking his course from the stars.

Bryce's horse was shod. His trail would be easy to pick up. His aim now was to get a long head start. He made a rough guess that the distance he'd have to cover would be seventy or eighty miles and he rode his horse accordingly.

Bryce welcomed the sunrise. He rode all the next day, halting an hour or two during the middle of the day. He saw scattered bunches of cattle and an occasional rider in the distance. Luck favored him and he came no closer than a mile to the nearest rider. He rode out of his way to avoid cow camps and ranches.

It was difficult to tell if the pair of riders he sighted behind him three or four times were cowboys after cattle or men trailing him. It didn't much matter because he was a long way ahead of them and he reckoned he would be reaching Applegate's ranch by dusk. He wondered if the pair of riders were the Avenging Angels, though he figured they'd be ahead of him and would be at the ranch with their loot when he got there.

Sundown found him in the broken country south of the Little Rockies. Long ridges spotted with scrub pines, long draws thick with brush. It was the fall of the year and the wild berries were ripe on the branches. He'd lean from his saddle and scoop a handful to satisfy the hunger that was beginning to bother him.

He topped a ridge and came on to a wagon trail. Five minutes later he was looking down on a small cluster of log buildings and corrals. He knew he had reached Wade Applegate's horse ranch.

No man challenged his approach, not even the barking of a dog. But he knew that he was being watched as he reined up in the slanting rays of sunset in front of a big log barn.

A tall, white-moustached man, with a six-shooter swinging low on his lean flank appeared in the doorway of the barn. His skin was leathery, seamed, stretched over a big boned, homely face. His deep-set eyes were dark brown, flecked with grey. He scrutinized Bryce closely.

'You are Bryce Bradford,' he said in a deep, soft-toned voice. 'You're the livin' image of your father. I've been expectin' you to show up here sooner or later. Get down and put up your horse.'

'There's two men here ahead of me?' questioned Bryce.

'Two men, yes. But keep your hand away from your gun. They've given their word. I want yours. This is not the time nor place for gun fightin'.'

Bryce dismounted. His hand was gripped so hard that he almost winced. Wade Applegate was sixty or more but he was hard as rawhide and his joints were limber.

'One of Pete Kaster's horses,' he said, reading the K brand on the sweat-streaked brown. 'A good one, but I raise better.' The man spoke without bragging. He was simply stating a fact.

When Bryce had unsaddled, watered and fed his horse, they walked together towards the house. As they went in, Bryce saw the two men he was looking for standing in front of the open fireplace, facing him.

The larger, older man had a black-spade beard streaked with white. His eyes were as cold and hard as grey steel. The younger man's eyes were crossed but of the same color. His hair was straight and coarse and black. They were undoubtedly father and son.

'The older man is Matthew,' Wade

Applegate introduced him to Bryce. 'The other is Stephen. Seven and Eleven!'

The Avenging Angels, according to the law at Rainbow's End, were allowed to keep their given names only. They were always referred to by number.

That they knew Bryce's identity was a foregone conclusion. They eyed him with cold enmity and he faced them with grim-lipped defiance. These were the two men who had been sent from Rainbow's End to track him down, but they had given their word to Wade Applegate that they would not stain his hospitality with bloodshed. Bryce was likewise bound.

Bryce had hung his hat on the elk antlers in the hall and had put his Winchester carbine in the gun rack that held a dozen rifles and carbines and two sawed-off double-barrelled shotguns. He had un-buckled his cartridge belt and hung it with his holstered six-shooter below his hat. He'd seen the two black hats and belts and guns on the rack that belonged to the two men.

'You two men,' Wade Applegate spoke to father and son, 'will use the attic room. The ladder is at the end of the hall. Supper will be on the table in an hour. That will give you ample time to wash up.'

Wade Applegate made no pretence about the broad hint. When they had left, Bryce turned to him and asked bluntly, 'What happened to my father, Bob Bradford? I've come a long ways to find out.'

'Bob Bradford is dead,' Applegate told him.

'Then he was murdered,' Bryce said tensely. 'Destroyed by the Avenging Angels of the Mormon Church.'

'Your father was shot down before he reached my place. The two Avenging Angels who had him prisoner, taking him to Fort Benson, were killed at the same time. All three men were on a stagecoach that was held up by road-agents on the night before Christmas one year ago. The stage was robbed and the three men murdered.'

Bryce sat stiffly, letting the truth sink in. Then he said, 'One thing I have to tell you now, sir.'

'If it concerns the stage hold-up and your being elected Sheriff of Buffalo Run, I am already aware of it,' Wade Applegate interrupted.

'Those two men told you?'

'No. They are bound by their oath to silence. I have other sources of information.'

'What crimes am I charged with, sir?'

Bryce asked. 'These men have been sent to track me down.'

'You'll hear the charges at sunrise. Until then, there will be no discussion under my roof.'

Bryce glanced quickly around the big square room. Fur rugs covered the floor. Books lined the shelves along the wall. A glass humidor was filled with coarse tobacco and a dozen pipes were in the rack on the home-made table that was piled with newspapers and periodicals.

'Your room is across the hall from mine, Bryce. Would you care for a drink of good whisky before you wash up?'

'I'm not much of a drinker,' admitted Bryce, 'but I need one to get the taste out of my mouth.'

Bryce didn't hear the squaw come in on moccasined feet. Her guttural voice behind him startled him. The meaningless string of cuss words that came from the scrubbed moon fare was even more startling.

'Leah has her likes and dislikes. She don't happen to like our other guests,' Wade Applegate explained.

'I hope I meet the test, sir,' Bryce said with a tentative smile.

'She knows something about you. Her sister works for Nile Carter at Buffalo Run.'

He showed Bryce his room and left him to wash up.

The squaw seemed to have outdone herself. Clean white sheets and pillow cases on the big bed. Wild roses in a glass jar on the dresser. A clean shirt, underwear and socks folded neatly on the bed. On the washstand there was a shaving mug and brush and open razor.

He was tucking in his clean shirt when he noticed a twice-folded envelope pinned inside the shirt pocket. There were two sheets of writing paper. One was the farewell letter from Bryce's father that he had forgotten to remove from the money belt he had left with Virginia Morgan. The other was a note from Nile Carter. It read:

Do not, under any circumstances, return to Buffalo Run, Bryce Bradford! The Stranglers here have tied your hangman's knot. Judge Plato Morgan and his daughter Virginia are leaving by stage for Fort Benton. I have persuaded Virginia to accept your generous gift.

Every man and woman in Buffalo Run has been commanded by Quensel to attend the funeral of Charlie Decker, shot down by the stranger from no-where.

As for me, Nile is still dealing at the El Dorado.

N.

Bryce put both letters in his pocket. The supper bell was ringing. His door opened and the younger one of the Avenging Angels stepped in and closed the door. 'We got a notion that Wade Applegate will clear you tomorrow,' he told Bryce. 'But we'll follow you to hell and bring you back to Rainbow's End, dead or alive.' He opened the door and walked out.

Bryce caught a glimpse of his own face in the mirror. He didn't like what he saw reflected there, a pair of cold eyes that held murder set in a greyish-green mask of bitter hatred.

'To hell with it,' he spoke aloud to the mirrored face, not knowing exactly what he meant.

He let himself out and walked down the hall. Wade Applegate and the two Avenging Angels were in the big room. Neither of the two men had changed clothes.

Applegate motioned them to their seats at a heavy plank table twenty feet long. Matthew sat at one end of the table, his son at his right. The host sat at the head with Bryce on his right.

Father and son commenced wolfing their food in a wordless, noisome exhibition of uncouth table manners. The food on platters and in bowls in front of them had been there for a long time, getting cold. The squaw brought in hot platters of steaming food and put them in front of Wade Applegate, then a big pot of hot black coffee.

Bryce had never tasted better food. The thick T bone steak covered the huge crockery plate, the mashed potatoes had a creamy color. The dutch-oven biscuits were hot to the touch, with wild strawberry syrup and home-made butter, and cream so thick you had to spoon it into the cup.

All men were welcome here. But those who came took whatever they got. Wade Applegate's squaw did the separating.

The four men finished supper in silence. Supper over, Bryce walked in the moonlight with his host in the lead. They came to a grassy clearing fenced in by a whitewashed rail fence. There were three grave mounds. One grave was marked by a large boulder on which was crudely chiselled the name ROBERT BRADFORD.

'I brought your father's body here for

burial, together with the bodies of the two Avenging Angels who had him under guard. I knew your father but the two others still remain without identity.'

'I don't know how to thank you, sir.' Bryce said, his voice choked. 'I can't find the right words.'

'No need to thank me. Your father was my friend.' Applegate put a hand on Bryce's shoulder. 'I had seventy-five thousand dollars in the strong-box on that stage. It was tithe money I owed the Mormon Church, consigned to the Bank at Fort Benton. Two masked road-agents held up the stage, killed the shotgun guard, the two Avenging Angels, and shot down your father who was unarmed. Only the stagedriver and one woman passenger were spared. The tithe money was stolen.'

Wade Applegate's handsome weathered face looked like it had been chiselled from grey granite.

'I am still held responsible for every dollar of that stolen money.' He gripped Bryce's arm. 'Matthew and Stephen have been sent here to collect that tithe. Tomorrow morning they will demand payment. Both of them are killers.'

'There were sixty thousand dollars in the strong-box they just robbed,' Bryce told him. 'They collected that tithe of yours in the same way your money was stolen. You don't owe them too much, sir.'

'They have not mentioned anything about robbing a strong-box,' said the older man.

Bryce told him about the cardboard signed by 7 and 11. 'They made it plain enough it was tithe collected. I followed their trail here,' Bryce told him.

'I'll bring up the matter of the robbery with them,' Applegate said grimly. 'Now concerning your trial tomorrow morning, Bryce, they will demand twenty-five years tithe owed by your father, and according to their rules, a son is held responsible for his father's debts.'

'My father held out tithe each year from his earnings,' Bryce said hotly, his temper rising. 'He kept it in a black satchel. He must have had it with him when he was killed. I have his letter to prove it.' Bryce took out the letter and handed it over.

'I was sent out as sheriff to fetch back the road-agents and the sixty thousand dollars they stole,' Bryce grinned twistedly. 'I aim to do just that.'

He shoved his hand into his pants pocket and crushed Nile's note into a crumpled ball and left it there.

Bryce told him about Stephen coming into his room and making the threat.

'I don't trust that unholy combination of father and son,' said Wade Applegate. 'They're an evil example of two generations of polygamous inbreeding. I was sent from Salt Lake City along with your father's father to guide those exiled outcasts to some isolated spot beyond the reach of the law of the United States. Those outcast Mormons set themselves apart as holy martyrs. I left them there and came to this place to lose my identity. So I have waited, even as your father waited, for the long arm of the Avenging Angels to reach me.'

'Did you know who those men were when you offered them welcome?' Bryce asked.

'I recognized the Square and Compass brand on their horses.'

'Then why?' Bryce asked.

'The sign above the gate that reads, "All men are welcome here. Let no man violate that trust".' The tall white-haired man smiled tolerantly.

The blast of gunfire punctuated whatever Bryce was about to say. He reached instinctively for his gun but the gun now hung on Wade Applegate's rack in the hall.

Applegate moved with silent swiftness. 'Follow me,' he whispered. He led Bryce along a trail to a camp of half a dozen tepees, where a number of squaws were busy around the campfires. Wade Applegate lifted the flap of a tepee and motioned Bryce inside. Glowing coals from a small fire in the center shed a red light inside. Wade Applegate lifted a buffalo robe and his hand came out holding a filled cartridge belt and holstered Colt pistol, which he handed to Bryce, saying, 'You might need it.'

The shooting puzzled Bryce. He was about to ask a question, but when the older man shook his head, the question died a slow death.

The echoes of the shots left a void of silence in the night. A silence charged with danger that tensed Bryce's muscles and screwed his nerves taut as tight-strung, thin wires.

As the two men stepped out of the tepee, the fat squaw came up at a jog trot. Anger blazed in her opaque black eyes as she talked to Applegate in Sioux. When she finished what seemed like an angry tirade, Applegate told Bryce what she'd said. That there were two dead men at the little graveyard, and that two horsebackers rode away after roping the sign over the gate and pulling it down.

Both dead men were strangers to Bryce, but Wade Applegate knew them. They both worked for Kaster and Fogarty.

Both men had been shot in the back as they stood, tracked in the dark shadows of the high willows and buck-brush. Neither man had been given an even chance, both guns were still in their holsters.

'There, but for the grace of God,' Wade Applegate said, 'lie the dead bodies of Bryce Bradford and Wade Applegate.'

'The pair of Avenging Angels?'

'Who else? The squaw said they saddled a couple of fresh horses and had them tied in the brush while I was showing you where your father was buried. The way I read the sign, the dead men were sent to trail you and while they stood in the brush undecided, Matthew and Stephen slipped up. Mistaking the shadowy forms for you and me, they carried out their orders of destruction, and are now on their way back to Rainbow's End, rejoicing.'

Wade Applegate led the way back to the house. When they had taken a drink together, Bryce told the older man that he'd like him to read his father's letter and another unfinished letter written by a range detective hired by the Wells Fargo Express Company, to investigate the recent hold-ups of the stage. He explained how the letter had dropped out of Quensel's pocket.

Wade Applegate read the first letter aloud in softened tone, while Bryce sat back with half closed eyes as the strange wording of the letter took on a meaning he could now comprehend.

Dear Son. By the time you read this I will be gone. After twenty-five years the Avenging Angels of the outcast Mormons of Rainbow's End have located me. They are taking me back to stand trial. I will be sentenced and shot down.

These two long riders have given me their sworn promise not to hunt down and destroy my son, on two conditions. First, that I pay them twenty-five years' tithe. Second, that I will take them to Wade Applegate's hideout.

I have the tithe money in a black satchel and am taking it along to Rainbow's End, but regarding Wade Applegate, it is a difficult decision to make.

If I take them to Wade's horse ranch where he has lived in safety all these years, it means the destruction of the best friend a man ever had. On the other hand, if I refuse to betray Wade Applegate, you will be shot down by the two Avenging Angels who are waiting outside while I write this farewell letter to you, my son. Forgive me if I refuse to betray my friend. Wait here at the ranch six months, Bryce. Then put your affairs in order and go to Wade Applegate, whose ranch you can find from the directions I gave you. He will know what to do. May God protect you, my son. Your father, Bob Bradford.

When the letter ended, there was a hushed silence. Both men felt the strange invisible shadow of Bob Bradford's presence in the big room.

'If he had only told me beforehand, given me some warning, told me what to do,' Bryce voiced his thoughts.

'Bob Bradford didn't know himself. A condemned man has no advance warning,' said Wade Applegate.

'I was across the border in Mexico bringing up a drive of cattle I had bought. When I got back to the ranch my father was gone. His letter was on the dresser in his bedroom, weighted down by his gun and cartridge belt.

'I waited six months for his return, then I sold the ranch and the stock. He'd told me to come first to the cowtown of Buffalo Run and make cautious inquiry regarding a squawman who raised Morgan horses. I hit the trail for Montana, travelling light and at night. When I reached Buffalo Run the Avenging Angels had two horses wearing the Square and Compass in the barn. They'd paid two weeks' board bill in advance and pulled out. But I'd already played the damn fool and shot down a tinhorn named Charlie Decker. After I was cleared of the killing, which was in self-defense, I was elected Sheriff of Buffalo Run. That night the stage was held up and I took the trail of the road-agents. When I went to the barn to get a horse, the two Square and Compass horses were gone.'

'Are you calculating on working at that sheriff's job?' Wade Applegate asked.

'Yes sir,' Bryce answered quickly. 'But there's a hangman's rope waiting for me if I have the damnfool guts to return to Buffalo Run.'

Bryce picked up the unfinished letter the detective had written. He handed it to Applegate to read.

When he finished reading it, there was a grim smile under the drooping moustache.

'This letter, properly presented in court,' he said, 'will hang Quensel and Fogarty and Kaster. I hope to be there when Judge Morgan passes his death sentence. Those three hangings should clear the air. Your sheriff's job is to cut out the pattern, a pattern cut on the bias if you capture the three alive.'

'It will take some tricky skull work,' Bryce said doubtfully. 'My brain don't work that way.'

'I'll be around to help you mark the cards and stack the deck. Quensel isn't the only gambler who can handle a double-shuffle.'

'I'd like to bring in the road-agents they sent me after, together with the loot,' Bryce grinned wolfishly.

'I thought you said your brain didn't function when it came to tricks. Fetch Matthew and Stephen in on the hoof, and you'll have pulled a couple of white rabbits from the plug hat.' Wade Applegate got up and filled two glasses from the whisky bottle. 'This calls for a drink, Sheriff.'

It was when Bryce set down his empty glass that he remembered what Nile had said in her note, that Judge Morgan and Virginia were leaving by stage for Fort Benton. His brows pulled together in a thoughtful scowl.

'Can I get a letter off right now by fast messenger?' he asked.

'An Injun boy can out-travel the Pony Express. Get the letter written.' Wade Applegate brought out pen and ink and writing paper.

Dear Nile. I hope this reaches you in time to keep Judge Plato Morgan in town. If my luck holds out, I'll bring in the road-agents to be tried in his court. Don't tell anyone but the Judge that I'm coming back. I'm trusting you, Nile, with all I got to lose. Bryce.

Wade Applegate's squaw was waiting when Bryce put the letter in an envelope and sealed it. She carried it outside to the Indian boy who sat bareback on one of the rancher's Morgan horses.

CHAPTER EIGHT

A man could buy anything at Chepete's Halfway House, providing he had the money.

That wily, weasel-eyed little French-Canadian half-breed had no fixed price on anything he had to sell in his trading store. Guns and ammunition had a varying value. The rot-gut whisky he made and peddled by the jug or bottle was priced according to the purchaser's urgent needs and the amount of money in his pocket. Everything Chepete had to sell was based on a varying scale.

Sometimes the price ran high, into real money, for such items as the dead body of a man you wanted killed and didn't want to get your own hands bloody. The little 'breed charged according to the danger involved in the actual killing and the risk afterwards.

A man couldn't be too careful and cautious about slip-ups and mistakes that might get him hung by the Vigilantes or shot down by a relative or friend of the murdered man, Chepete would explain it with gestures to a prospective customer.

'Cash on de barrel-head, by Gar.' Chepete's beady black eyes would bore tiny gimlet holes through a man to read the thoughts in his brain. 'Of course,' he would shrug his buckskin shoulders by way of emphasis, 'there would be a bullet left hin de gon for dat man who say he hire dis Chepete. Mebbe dat man talk lak de magpie with de split tongue when dat man she'll get dronk. Hor mebbe talk in de sleep, han de woman hin de blanket listen. Bimeby dat gossip she spread lak damn prairie fire hin de dry grass. Me, Chepete, Hi'm tak no damn chances, by Gar.'

It was rumoured that Chepete was in the habit of using that second bullet more often than not. His trade in that commodity, involving danger and risk, had fallen off.

The selling of information was another item that was apt to be costly in Chepete's fluctuating scale of prices. It all depended on what a customer wanted to find out and the danger involved.

Chepete's knowledge of what had happened in the past, what was going on now and what was likely to happen in the future was a vast storehouse, kept behind the cunning half-breed's sealed lips. Money was the only key that could unlock his lipless mouth that opened and closed like the jaws of a trap. The grin on his lean, hatchet face was wolfish. His laugh had the sound of a trap chain rattling. His movements were as swift and furtive as the weasel eyes. Chepete was a fast man with a knife or gun or with the three foot length of greased buckskin string looped around his lean middle under the multi-colored woven Hudson's Bay sash he wore, the long fringes of which hung down on one side where he wore his knife scabbard.

Chepete stood five feet in his Cree moccasins. He could stand flat-footed and kick the ash off a cigarette in the mouth of a six-foot man. Or his moccasined foot could break the Adam's apple in a man's throat or break a man's jaw. Sometimes he used both feet to kick a man in the belly or guts or lower down. The little half-breed could handle himself in the toughest company.

It was only on very rare occasions he ever had need to call upon the backing of the score or more 'breeds who camped down the creek with their wives and families. French-Canadian 'breeds like himself who had followed their leader when they had been run across the line under the armed escort of the Northwest Mounted Police. The Canadian government had weeded Chepete and his followers out as undesirables as the aftermath of the Riel Rebellion.

Whenever the notion came, Chepete would 'mak de dance'. All that it took to make a dance was a fiddle and a jug and cornmeal sprinkled on the smooth worn pineboard floor of the log cabin store.

Usually the notion came when Chepete was pleased about something that had put money in his iron safe or benefited his greed for power. He'd uncork his jug and drink till the desire to dance the Red River jig set fire to his blood.

There was such a dance now in full swing at Chepete's Halfway House when the pair of Avenging Angels, Matthew and Stephen, rode up out of the night. They reined up and leaning across their saddlehorns, they peered into the lantern lit room through the open door.

A dozen couples were dancing to the fast beat of the Red River jig. The fiddler stood on a long platform, fiddle tucked under his chin, the resined bow moving swiftly.

Chepete leaped high above the floor, kicking his moccasined heels together. He bounced like a rubber ball, his body twisting backwards in a somersault that landed him on his feet. The shrill laughter of the young 'breed girls could be heard through the shouted acclamation of the men.

Quickly Chepete motioned the fiddler to continue playing. He threaded his way with darting movements through the open door, flattening himself outside in the dark shadow of the log wall, all in a matter of seconds.

'Sacre!' The half-breed's voice knifed through the noise from inside. 'She's de 'breed dance, by Gar. What you want at Chepete's, eh?'

It was not the first time that white men with rotgut whisky burning their guts had showed up to break up the 'breed dances at Chepete's Halfway House. Pete Kaster's tough crew of cowpunchers would swarm into dance with the pretty 'breed girls, shoving the men aside. Sometimes it would be Tim Fogarty's bullwhackers and mule skinners. Again it would be a rowdy hoodlum gang of young toughs from Buffalo Run, come to break up the dance.

The results were always the same. A general ruckus, a free for all fight. Knives would cut and slash and stab. Pistols would be drawn and fired. Women would scream and run to hide in the brush.

The drunken white men would prowl the brush, pulling young 'breed girls from their hiding places, their dresses ripped off.

Chepete's trading store would be a blood-spattered shambles. His stock of rotgut white mule corn whisky would be stolen, jugs and bottles smashed. Breaking up the 'breed dances came under the head of indoor sports. Gangs of horsebackers thought nothing of a thirty-forty mile ride to join the festivities.

There was a Colt .45 in Chepete's hand as he stood crouched in the shadows.

'We been here before, Chepete,' Matthew said. 'All we want is a place to lay low for a few days, maybe a week. The same as we did before.'

'Oui, by Gar,' Chepete grinned to himself. 'Ride to the barn, put hup de horse. Hi'm show hup soon.'

'Don't tell anybody we're here, Chepete,' Matthew warned him in a saw-edged whisper. 'Fetch me a jug, the best you got. I got money to pay.'

Stephen was bent low along the neck of his horse. His bloodshot crossed eyes had a lustful glassy look as he watched a slim half-breed girl in a red dress and beaded moccasins dancing with a tall, wide-shouldered 'breed in his early twenties.

The tall 'breed was laughing as he swung the girl off the floor. Her skirt swirled up to show brown-skinned, shapely bare legs. Her hair hung down her back in a blue-black mane and her white teeth flashed in a smile, her large brown eyes soft, melting.

'Fetch me that 'breed girl in the red dress, Chepete,' Stephen's voice was thick-tongued, slobbery.

'I bring you one other girl, eh?' Chepete told him.

'I picked the one I want,' Stephen said in a surly voice.

'I bring two, t'ree girls,' Chepete said uneasily. 'You take your pick. Keep all t'ree, eh?'

Stephen's gun was in his hand. 'I told you the one in red dress.'

Matthew spurred his horse into Stephen's and took the gun away. 'We can't afford a ruckus here. Git that into your rutty-brained skull. Pull up the slack in your jaw and wipe your chin off.' Matthew's voice was that of a father speaking to a half-witted son.

'Everything you own has a price, Chepete,' Matthew said. 'Fetch the girl in the red dress to the barn and I'll pay you what she's worth.'

'Qui, by Gar,' Chepete said, shrugging his shoulders.

'Send a man you can trust,' Matthew lowered his voice to a whisper, 'to Wade Applegate's ranch, to pick up what news there is to be gathered. If you don't have a man you can trust, go yourself. I'll make it worth your while, Chepete.'

'Dat Big Gregory,' a sly grin crossed Chepete's face, 'he dance with my girl Marie in de red dress. Sacre, Hi'm mark half de Gregory's debt off de ledger. When he ride hoff, I bring Marie to de barn. One hondred dollars.' He drove his bargain.

'Fifty when you fetch the girl,' Matthew dickered shrewdly, 'fifty when Gregory brings back the news from Applegate's.'

'She's de bargeen! Sacre, damn!' Chepete's chuckle had a dry rattling sound. He motioned the two men away.

Stephen was once more bent over his saddle watching every movement of the girl's lithe, slim body, the bright colored beads on her moccasins sparkling like jewels on her dancing feet.

Matthew crowded his horse close. There was a snarl in his rasping whisper. 'Last time you got outa hand, I tied you up. Git your mind off it!' The quirt in his hand made a hissing sound as it fell across the back of Stephen's horse. For a few seconds, Stephen had all he could do to stay in the saddle.

They rode at a lope towards the big barn and its hayloft hiding place.

CHAPTER NINE

Bryce Bradford and Wade Applegate were up before sunrise, leading the horses in the barn to water at the creek, cleaning the stalls, haying and graining the horses, when Big Gregory showed up.

The two men watched the tall half-breed ride through the gate and come down the hill.

'One of Chepete's 'breed outfit,' the squawman said, 'and up to no good.'

'Long time no see, Gregory,' Wade Applegate said. 'I hear you're going to marry Marie, Chepete's youngest.'

Gregory grinned uneasily, shifting his weight to one stirrup. 'Maybe we get married purty quick now.'

'You're a good picker,' Applegate said. 'Step down. What's on your mind, besides your guilty conscience?'

The big 'breed scuffed his new boots in the dust. Tiny beads of sweat began to show on his high cheekbones as he scowled at the ground in a long, uneasy silence.

'Chepete,' Gregory met the older man's eyes, 'he sent me over here to find out things. Said for me to hang around and listen to any talk and keep my eyes open and my mouth shut. Two white men Chepete had hid in the hayloft will pay me when I get back with the news.'

Wade Applegate cut a meaning look at Bryce, then he spoke to Gregory. 'Did you see the two men? Did one have grey whiskers, the other about your age?'

'Yes, sir. They rode up about midnight. Chepete called me from the dance and said he was hiding the two men out for a few days. They were in the hayloft when I saddled my horse to come here. I got a look at their horses, branded with a brand I never seen.' He squatted on his boot-heels and picked up a stick. He drew the Square and Compass in the dirt.

Wade Applegate told Gregory to put up his horse and come to the house. When the 'breed came from the barn, they started towards the house by way of the graveyard.

'I come here,' the half-breed said, 'to sneak around and find out things. By rights, you should run me off. What are you going to do to me?'

'Nothing. On the way to the house I'll show you two dead men under a tarp. The bodies of Wade Applegate and Bryce Bradford. They were both shot in the back by the two men hiding in the hayloft. The men who rode those Square and Compass horses. You will take the information back to Chepete.'

They went into the house by way of the kitchen door where the squaw was getting breakfast. She eyed the half-breed Cree with cold suspicion. She was a full-blood Sioux and the Sioux and Crees had been old enemies before the coming of the white man. Now the Sioux and Crees were conquered people under the thumb of the white man and the United States Government.

'Keep your scalping knife in its scabbard, woman,' Wade Applegate told his squaw. 'Big Gregory is fixing to get married and he needs his hair left on.'

He led the way to the lean-to shed at the kitchen door where all three of them washed up at the scoured tin basin, drying on the same clean roller towel.

Wade Applegate was relying on his squaw's curiosity and it amused him to watch the way she maneuvered it, detaining Gregory in the kitchen while Bryce and he sat down to breakfast in the dining-room. Before long they heard them talking in a conglomeration of Sioux, Cree and white man's swear words, with a little sign language to bridge the gaps.

The squawman interpreted the talk as he unscrambled it for Bryce's benefit. 'She hates Chepete's guts, but feels sorry for his Cree woman. Chepete's twin daughters work in the trading store. Antoinette, the smart one, keeps the books and handles the men. Marie is quiet and gentle. Both are good-looking girls. Antoinette takes after her father, cunning and treacherous. Chepete has taught her a lot of tricks. She's too handy with a knife. She's never been married to any of the men she's strung along and she's had a lot of 'em. She's a young wildcat, the one called Toni for short. Purrs like a kitten under a man's caresses, while she goes through his pockets. If she's caught, she claws and bites her way out. You see some gent looks like he's tried to tame a wildcat, after he's spent an evenin' with Toni.

'My woman is giving some advice to Gregory. She just told him she'll cut his gizzard out if he ever hurts Marie.'

Big Gregory's face was red when he came to the table. He sat opposite Bryce but was too self-conscious to help himself to the food.

'Tie into that grub before it gets cold,' Wade Applegate told him. 'Clean your plate, or my squaw is apt to scalp you.'

He said conversation ruined a good meal. The table talk should be limited to 'Pass the salt.'

When the meal was finished, they went into the living-room and when comfortably seated, the squawman spoke through his pipe smoke. 'How soon does Chepete expect you back, Gregory?'

'He said the two white men were anxious to get the news I was to fetch back. He was charging them plenty, but they wouldn't pay till I got back. The sooner I get back the quicker he'll get his money and mark my debt off the ledger.'

'Did he know who the men were?'

'He said they were road-agents who held up the stage two nights ago.'

'Did Chepete offer to cut you in on any deal?'

'You know how Chepete is,' Gregory said uneasily. 'He talks a lot without saying anything.' The young 'breed was beginning to sweat a little.

Bryce knew that it had to be fear of some kind that was holding him back from talking. Bryce felt a little sorry for him. In spite of his better judgment, he had taken a liking to the 'breed.

'How many times, Gregory,' Wade

Applegate asked quietly, 'have you helped Chepete with his chores?'

'Chepete has me across the barrel,' the words were forced out. 'He lets me go in debt at the store. I owe him for a Miles City saddle that costs forty dollars. A pair of chaps. A silver mounted bit and spurs, a Stetson hat. I wanted to make a showing so Marie would like me.' Gregory was sitting on the edge of his chair, hands clenched. Wade Applegate let him sweat.

'Chepete let you get over your head in debt,' he finally said. 'Then what happened?' The softness in his lazy drawl was no longer there.

'You know what happened then,' Gregory exclaimed. 'I was one of the 'breeds Chepete sent to steal twenty-five head of your yearling colts from the weanling herd at Haystack Butte.' His voice cracked and broke on a high note.

'Why didn't you call me in last fall with the other 'breeds you brought here for punishment?' he asked.

'I had my own reasons, Gregory. The others were old offenders. I let them off easy and told them what would happen if I ever caught any of them again stealing my stock.'

The 'breed wiped the sweat from his face

with the back of his hand. Wade Applegate's eyes were cold as blue ice.

'Before Chepete sent you here, Gregory,' he said. 'He made you a proposition. What was it?'

'He said the two men he was hiding out had a lot of money in a canvas bean sack. He saw them take it up the ladder to the hayloft. Chepete said he was going to get that money they stole when they held up the stage. He said he'd have them dead drunk by dark tonight and he wanted me there to back his play if he got into a tight. He said they were killers. He said he'd cut me in on the money. He had me over the barrel,' Gregory whined.

'So you took him up on the proposition.' Wade Applegate's voice was gentle.

'He had a knife in his hand,' the 'breed said. 'I had to agree. I was sick with fear. He told me to saddle up and ride here. He said the two men had killed you and the new sheriff of Buffalo Run. He wanted to make sure you were both dead.'

'What else?'

'He said those two road-agents had propositioned him to hire a few 'breeds and run your horses south. Chepete said if I helped him kill the two men in the hayloft, there was nothing to stop us from stealing your horses and he'd cut me in on the profits.'

'It must have been a surprise to find us alive,' Wade Applegate said, his hard lips twisting in a sardonic grin.

'Yes, sir, it was, but I was glad to see you both alive.' Gregory rose to his feet and stood there wiping the sweat from his face with his shirt sleeve.

Applegate let him stand while he filled his pipe from a buckskin pouch. When he got the tobacco lit, he smoked for a while in thoughtful silence. In the early morning sunlight that came into the room through an open window a meadow-lark warbled its song from a tree top.

Bryce looked at the tall young half-breed, dressed in a bright red shirt and new pants and new squeaky boots. Humili-ation was clearly stamped on his face as he waited with quivering belly to receive whatever punishment was meted out.

When the song of the meadow-lark ended, Wade Applegate spoke.

'All you've really done, Gregory,' he said, 'is to confess the crimes Chepete had in mind, so supposing you return to Chepete's place and tell him you saw Wade Applegate and Sheriff Bryce Bradford lying dead under a bloodstained old wagon tarp at the end of the graveyard. Tell Chepete that and nothing more. Whatever you do after that is strictly up to you, Gregory.'

Bryce had got to his feet and stood facing the 'breed to whom he said, 'Wade Applegate is giving you a chance to prove yourself, Gregory. He's giving you a chance to marry your girl.'

Gregory's sagging shoulders straightened and he looked into the squawman's steady blue eyes.

'I'll do whatever you tell me to, Mister Wade,' he said humbly.

'All you have to do is to take a few lies back, Gregory,' Applegate told him, then asked, 'How much do you owe Chepete?'

'Almost a hundred dollars. Toni showed me the ledger. But I got to pay him two hundred that isn't on the books.'

'What for?'

'If I don't pay him the two hundred dollars, he won't let me marry Marie. That's the price he has on Marie.'

Wade Applegate crossed the room to the roll top desk in the far corner of the room. A moment later he returned with a roll of bills. 'Here's three hundred, Gregory. That'll get you off the hook.'

'I can't take money from you, Mister

Wade, unless you let me work it out.'

'If that's the way you feel about it, I'll give you the contract for putting up the hay. I'll furnish the teams and mowing machines and hay wagons. You hire what men you'll need and I'll pay them their wages.' Wade Applegate smiled. 'Get Marie away from Chepete's and bring her here. That woman of mine will take good care of her. When the haying's done I'll need a man in that winter line camp. You can move in there with your bride. You've got a job with me as long as you want it, Gregory.'

'You mean,' Big Gregory forced a wry grin. 'that you're trusting me?'

'Why not? That woman of mine claims you're a good man even if you got some Cree blood in you. I've never yet known her judgment to be wrong.'

Gregory was caught off-balance by Wade Applegate's understanding and generosity, and Bryce Bradford was sharing his emotions as they both looked at the white-haired man.

Wade Applegate seemed a little embarrassed by the frank admiration in the eyes of the two younger men. He looked at the clock on the mantelpiece. 'It's time for you to get going, Gregory.'

Big Gregory grinned widely and shook

hands awkwardly with them both. They watched him ride away.

'I reckon,' Bryce said quietly, 'it's about time for me to saddle up and hit the trail.'

'You realize the danger that lies in wait, Bryce. Take care of yourself. This is your home. Come back to it.' The blue eyes were misted with unshed tears, and Bryce knew that there would be a prayer in the older man's heart as he rode away.

CHAPTER TEN

Bryce Bradford was timing his arrival at Chepete's Halfway House for sometime after dark. He had given Big Gregory more than a half hour's head start. The young half-breed must have kept up a long trot because Bryce had not caught even a distant glimpse of the rider.

Bryce tried to figure out some plan as he rode along. He told himself all he had to do was hold back and wait for Chepete to make his killer-play for the loot. Let wolf eat wolf, then when the gunsmoke cleared and the dust settled, he could pick up the kindling. That was, Bryce told himself, what the average sheriff on a man hunt would do, play both ends against the middle. It would save a lot of wear and tear on the system.

But Bryce wasn't going into this in the capacity of a law officer. Matthew and his cross-eyed son were the Avenging Angels who had hounded his tracks. They'd shot down two men in the dark, believing they were killing Bryce Bradford and Wade Applegate, who never in his life had packed a gun. So Bryce wasn't going to let Chepete or any other man on earth do his gun chores for him.

He decided there was no use in mapping out any plan of attack until he got there. By the time he reached Chepete's Big Gregory would have delivered the news and no one would be expecting him to show up.

The rolling prairie had flattened out at late dusk. The shadows of night were blanketing the sage-brush and greasewood wasteland of Alkali Flat. Chepete's place was at the far end where the stage road crossed Alkali Creek.

Bryce took his bearings from the evening star. A big yellow lop-sided moon pushed up over the skyline as he was crossing the five mile stretch of Alkali Flat, and a prairie wolf somewhere in the night sat on gaunt haunches, long nose pointed skyward, and gave voice in a salute before starting its night prowl.

The wolf howl had no echo in the flat country, except in the heart of Bryce Bradford who knew the danger he was riding into, his hand on his gun, his hat slanted to throw his face in shadow.

Ahead showed the yellow blobs of light of Chepete's Halfway House. As he rode up, everything was quiet and peaceful and there was no sign of life anywhere. The double doors of the barn were closed, the door of the hayloft open. Bryce rode up from the blind end and swung down, dropping his bridle reins to ground-tie his horse.

He kept close to the shadows of the barn as he edged along, his gun ready. Every nerve in his body was taut as he shoved one of the big doors inward, wide enough to slip through. He stood flattened against the door he had closed, listening, eyes squinted into the darkness. The wooden butt of his Colt .45 felt moist in the sweaty palm of his hand.

He could hear the movements of the horses in their stalls but that was all. He was about to move when a dry scuffling came from the hayloft and particles of dust and hay came down into his eyes as he looked up.

'Quit that clawin' and bitin',' Stephen's voice had a nasal whine. 'Open them purty lips so's a man can pour some of your old man's rotgut into you. I'm fillin' that little belly of yours full of booze to set your guts afire and maybe you'll listen to reason and quit clawing me. I'll get you so drunk you can't move, you little bitch.'

'Hand me the jug. I'll do my own drinking,' the girl said. 'It won't be the first time I've drunk Papa's rotgut. Quit pawing me. I'll give in when I'm ready. . . .'

Bryce's eyes had focused to the dark. He could make out the ladder rungs nailed to the log wall and was edging his way cautiously across the hard-packed dirt floor when he heard a dull crashing noise above, like a man had fallen heavily.

Stephen's harsh outcry saw-edged inside the barn. Then bare or moccasined feet padded swiftly across the hayloft, then ceased abruptly. Then cowhide boots thumped overhead and Stephen spat out a string of obscenities.

Stephen was coming down the ladder now. Bryce, crouched to one side in the dark, waited until his feet touched the floor, then he was on his back, pitching him forward on his face.

Bryce grabbed at the shock of sweat matted hair and jerked Stephen's head around, twisting his face up to look into the cross-eyes. 'Know me, you slimy bastard? I'm Bryce Bradford!'

The gun slashed down in short chopping blows on the unprotected face and Stephen's high-bridged nose flattened out, spurting blood. His scream was choked off as Bryce's gun smashed the discolored yellow teeth into a gaping maw.

Bryce let go the sweaty hair. He shoved Stephen's battered, bloody face into the dirt, then got to his feet. He rolled Stephen over on his back and kicked him roughly in the crotch. Stephen let out one agonized scream, then was silent.

Darkness concealed the hate that masked Bryce's face as he stood straddle of the Avenging Angel from Rainbow's End. He was breathing heavily as he waited for the tight, twisted knot inside his belly to loosen.

Low, moaning sounds came from inside the barn and it took Bryce a little while to locate Big Gregory in the last empty stall. His hands were tied behind his back and his legs tied with a halter rope. When Bryce cut him free and struck a match, he saw the battered face of the big half-breed, who looked up at him from swollen slits of eyes.

'Marie,' Gregory's voice was a croaking whisper. 'Chepete sold her to the old man with the chin whiskers. He bought her for his son.'

'I'll get her for you, Gregory', Bryce told him. 'Just take it easy. Who worked you over?'

'Chepete and the old man were in the saloon drinking whisky. I told them you and Wade Applegate were both dead and I gave Chepete the money. I said I was taking Marie away tonight. The old man laughed and said his son had Marie in the hayloft.

'I ran for the barn. Chepete jumped my back as I was opening the barn door. He kicked me in the face and belly, then everything went black. I got to find Marie,' he croaked in a racking sob, and struggled to his feet.

Bryce led him to the front end of the barn and eased him down to a sitting position with his back against a manger. Stephen lay near the ladder, out like a light. 'Take it easy till I get back. Ride herd on that bastard. If he comes alive, yell for me.'

Bryce went up into the loft. It was empty. When he looked out the loft door he could see the girl on the ground in a motionless, twisted shape.

It was a fifteen foot drop from the loft to the ground. Bryce hung by his hands for a moment, then let go. He kept his body relaxed so that his knees hinged when he struck ground. He let himself go and rolled over and on to his feet almost on top of the girl.

Her head jerked up. For a brief instant Bryce got a look at the white face and the black fire in her wide eyes. Then her fingers were clawing at his face. He made an instinctive grab at her shoulders, pulling her close against him, lowering his head to protect his face.

'Take it easy,' Bryce told her as her clawlike fingers grabbed his hair and yanked. 'I'm not Stephen. I'm not going to hurt you. I'm taking you to Gregory.'

The girl was fighting like a young she-wildcat. Her teeth bit into the side of his neck and as he lifted his head, she spat a mouthful of his own blood in his face.

'Quit it,' Bryce panted, getting a grip of her long black hair to hold her face away. 'I came to take you to Gregory. Can't you get that through your head? I'm here to help you both, Marie.'

The black fire died out slowly in her eyes. She was no longer fighting, but the tenseness was still present.

'Who are you?' she asked.

'Bryce Bradford. You don't know me.'

'The new Sheriff at Buffalo Run?' she whispered tensely.

'I reckon so.' He forced a grin as he let go her hair.

'You're a liar, mister. Bryce Bradford is

dead. Those two men shot him and Wade Applegate at the squawman's horse ranch.'

'This is no time to argue with a woman,' Bryce said. He picked her up in his arms, expecting the clawing and biting to start again, but she made no effort to resume her wildcat tactics. Her body felt limp as she let her head fall back, her long hair almost touching the ground. Her large eyes were black depthless pools. The color was back in her face and in the red lips that parted in a smile. Then her arms went around his neck and she pulled his head down, fastening her lips on his.

Her teeth bit into his lip. Bryce felt his knees tremble. He had to tighten his arms to keep her twisting body from slipping. The blood was pounding into his throat, hammering against his eardrums. Her clinging mouth slid away and he heard her soft mocking laugh as he pushed the barn door open and carried her inside, kicking the door shut.

'Here's your girl,' Bryce told Gregory as he slid the girl down beside him. 'Take her. I got a job to do.'

'Marie.' The name was ripped from inside Gregory as he stumbled to his feet.

'I'm Toni,' the girl said. 'Marie's hid out. I put on her red dress. Cross-eyes didn't know the difference. Who's the man who carried me in?'

'Bryce Bradford,' Gregory said dazedly.

'Oh,' the girl's voice had a hint of defiance in it. 'I'm sorry I called you a liar, Sheriff.'

Bryce opened the door. 'Don't let Stephen get away,' he warned as he went out and closed the door.

Bryce was still trembling as he headed for the saloon, keeping close to the shadows of the buildings as he ran. He lifted the door latch slowly, then shoved the door open and stood back from it, his gun in his hand. When he peered into the lamplit room, the saloon was empty. He headed for the store and flattening himself against the log wall, he looked in through an unwashed window.

The small statured, wiry built man in the buckskin shirt squatted in front of the big black safe, working the combination, had to be Chepete.

Bryce made out the lanky, rawboned figure who stood back in the shadow beyond reach of the glow of the lamp on the counter above Chepete's head. Matthew's thin lips were skinned back and his pale eyes slivered. The gun in his hand moved a little in a short gesture as Chepete swung open the safe door.

'Dig into 'er, you runty bastard. I want all you got.' Matthew's short laugh sounded like seeds rattling in a dry gourd. 'Put the money in that sack I gave you and hurry it up. Me'n Stephen is pullin' out directly he gets his ashes hauled.'

Matthew moved out from the shadow and came slowly across the floor to approach the squatting Chepete from behind.

Chepete was working in feverish haste to fill the sack. His head kept twisting around as Matthew came towards him, his grey chin whiskers jutted out and murder in his eye.

'The safe, she's hempty, by Gar.' Chepete's head twisted upward. 'Hall de money I got in de worl' ees een dat sack.'

'You won't need money where you're goin', you runty 'breed.' Matthew grinned as he thumbed back the gun hammer.

Bryce's six-shooter barrel smashed the window-pane, whirling Matthew around. In that same split-second Chepete came up from the floor as if his legs were levered springs. His wiry little body twisted in mid-air and his moccasined feet struck Matthew full in the face just as the gun spat flame.

The kick slapped Matthew's head back

on its skinny neck. His long legs gave way and as he went over backwards a flailing arm knocked the lamp off the counter. The next instant there was a sheet of flame, ceiling high.

Chepete grabbed up the canvas sack of money from the floor and bent over, he moved swiftly, crabwise towards the back door. His face was a ghastly, slimy mask, the beady black eyes burning in deep sockets.

Bryce smashed the window in and threw one leg across the sill. If he moved fast he could drag Matthew out the back door Chepete had left open, before the place became an inferno.

He was less than twenty feet from Matthew, whose head was twisted sideways on its broken neck, his gun still gripped in his hand. Matthew's eyes opened and into their hate-glazed depths came recognition of Bryce Bradford. No muscle moved in the inert body and the hand holding the gun was rigid. Bryce wasn't aware that the six-shooter was cocked until flame spurted from its black muzzle.

Bryce shot at that instant, tearing a black hole above Matthew's high-bridged nose. Death fixed the hate in Matthew's eyes.

The bullet that had creased Bryce's ribs

was like a hot branding-iron. He staggered forward a step, then caught his balance. He was wading in a puddle of flames and smoke choked his throat. He grabbed Matthew by the feet and dragged him as he backed out the door and fell down the three steps to the ground, pulling the dead man clear.

Bryce coughed as he crawled away from the burning building. The flames licked the dry log walls and the exploding stock of cartridges stored inside the store sounded as if a gun battle was being waged.

Bryce saw Chepete bent over double as he carried the money sack to the log cabin where he lived with his squaw and two daughters.

The cabin door was open and the squaw stood motionless in the doorway, watching Chepete, but making no effort to lend her husband a helping hand, even when he stumbled and fell to the ground.

Chepete was spewing out a strange mixture of Canuck French and Cree blasphemy as he sat up, blood spilling from clenched teeth and down the corners of his ghastly grin. The sack was slowly spreading with crimson stain from the gunshot Matthew's bullet had torn.

Big Gregory ran out of the barn into the red glow of the fire. He called for Marie over and over with each unsteady, lurching step, like a mechanical man-sized talking toy.

Bryce stood facing the barn. He was squinting sweat from his eyes when he saw Stephen spur his horse out of the barn, a short-barrelled Winchester carbine gripped in both hands. The Square and Compass gelding was gun broke, trained by expert hand, and savvied the pressure of its rider's knees like the touch of a bridle rein.

Stephen charged his horse at Bryce, to ride him down. 'Stay dead!' he shouted. 'This time stay dead, Bryce Bradford!' Bryce felt the whining snarl of the 30-30 bullet past his head as the big gelding swerved sideways to avoid trampling Bryce, which is a horse's natural instinct unless it happens to be an outlaw horse turned man killer.

The sudden sideways jump of the horse threw Stephen off balance, making him grab the saddlehorn with one hand. Bryce shot at the quick moving target but missed.

Stephen suddenly let go the saddle gun and his hand slipped its frantic grip on the horn. As he fell, his boot caught in the ox-bow stirrup and a terror-filled scream came from his gaping mouth as he hung by one foot.

Then the scream was blotted out by a shod hoof as the running horse kicked loose. The momentum rolled his body over so that it lay face down, and it was then that Bryce saw the buckhorn haft and a few inches of steel of the bowie knife between the dead man's shoulder blades.

Bryce gulped down mouthfuls of clean fresh air as he fought back the nausea. He was moving like a sleep walker through the fire glow of his nightmare. The taste of death was in his mouth and the blast of gunfire was an aching drum in his brain. He forced himself to keep moving.

Somewhere beyond the barn lay the creek. He'd keep going until he found it. Never had water seemed more precious. The smoke-coated thickness of his tongue had swollen like a mouthful of dirty flannel, and as the waves of nausea came his eyes no longer focused. Only the will to get to water kept him on his feet.

He neither saw nor heard the girl in the torn red dress take hold of his arm and guide him. She held on to him while he sat belt deep in the water and lowered his head and face into the creek. Consciousness returned slowly and he became aware of somebody holding him, to keep him from toppling.

Bryce twisted his head around to see who it was. The half-breed girl was almost waist deep in the water, her red dress clinging wetly to her slim body. With the red glow of the blaze reflected on the water, she looked like a pagan goddess of fire standing in a river of molten flame that was by some conjuring trick, cooling. The deep black fire in her eyes held him trapped in a strange, gripping nightmare of unreality.

Bryce became dimly aware of men shouting and the resined scrape of a bow across fiddle strings while the fiddle was being tuned, then the quickened sound of the Red River Jig.

The spell was broken. 'Nero fiddled while Rome burned,' Bryce spoke without thinking.

Toni let go her hold on his shoulders. 'Stay where you are, mister, while I get your horse. I kept your gun dry. It's on the bank with your cartridge belt and hat. You're getting the hell away from here before those half-breed cronies Chepete left behind get drunk and start prowling. They don't like the color of a white man's skin around here.'

Bryce watched her wade through the shallow water and vanish from sight in the tall willows. He crawled up on the bank and sat down to drain the water from his boots, shivering a little as the night breeze penetrated his wet clothes.

He put on his hat and buckled on his cartridge belt, feeling the reassuring weight of his gun. Remembering he had fired it, he ejected the empty shells and shoved in fresh cartridges. Then he worked his way cautiously through the willow thicket and tangled underbrush, to get a look at what was going on.

Beyond reach of the heat from the still burning log building, Bryce could see the younger 'breeds with girls in their arms, dancing around a barrel of whisky that had been rolled out from the saloon. A pile of tin cups were in a bushel basket nearby. The fiddler stood on the whisky barrel, his fiddle tucked under his chin, the dancers moving in quick step.

Men, women and children were standing in family groups watching the dancers, while a group of several young 'breeds were drinking from a passed jug in the barn doorway. They were all armed and their saddled horses stood ground tied. The bodies of Matthew and Stephen still lay on the ground.

Bryce sought in vain for a glimpse of Big Gregory. Chepete's body was gone and his squaw was nowhere in sight.

Despite the fiddle music and the shrill squealing of the 'breed girls as their partners swung them off their feet, there was an undercurrent of tenseness beneath the surface of gaiety. A potential danger that formed a black whirlpool in the armed group of younger 'breeds. It was only a matter of time until the rotgut started working and then all hell would tear loose.

The sound of breaking brush on the far side of the creek turned Bryce around, his thumb on his gun hammer.

'Move fast, mister,' Toni's voice was sharp edged. 'Get over here.' She had on a shirt and overalls and her hair was piled up under the high crown of a wide-brimmed black hat. A filled cartridge belt sagged around her slim waist and she was mounted on Stephen's Square and Compass horse. She led Bryce's saddled horse by the bridle reins.

Bryce waded to the other side of the creek and stood close to her horse's withers. 'Chepete's cronies are holding a wake. Get a-horseback, mister.' Her red lips peeled back to show her teeth.

Bryce noticed the bloodstained canvas sack she had tied to the back of Stephen's saddle. When Bryce made a tentative gesture to re-tie a loosened string, and she slid a wet moccasined foot from the stirrup and without any indication of warning, kicked him, flat footed, in the face. It was more like a quick shove than a kick, but hard enough to send Bryce back a step, off-balance.

'Hands off, mister,' the 'breed girl's voice had a cat-like snarl.

Bryce was looking into the black muzzle of a Colt pistol in her hand. The black flame was in her eyes.

'It's mine,' she spat the words in his face. 'I earned every rotten dollar of it.'

'I don't want your damn money,' Bryce said. 'I was just going to tie a saddle string that came loose.' He turned his back on her and reached for the latigo strap to tighten his saddle cinch.

'I didn't see any sign of Gregory,' Bryce said over his shoulder. 'Did he get Marie and pull out?'

'To hell with that big ox and that cry-baby Marie. When I told him where I'd hid her, he left the barn like a turpentined dog.'

She shoved the gun back into its holster

and twisted sideways in the saddle to tie the sack on securely.

'I'm getting to hell and gone away from here,' she whispered from behind clenched teeth. 'Get a-horseback, like I said.'

'I'm staying behind,' Bryce told her. 'I got a couple of chores to finish at Chepete's place.'

'What about the money?' the girl asked.

'As Sheriff of Buffalo Run I set out to fetch back a couple of road-agents who held up the stage and got away with a lot of money. I'm taking their dead bodies back.'

"What about the money?' the girl asked.

'It's hidden somewhere,' Bryce eyed the girl narrowly. 'I'll prowl around till I locate it.'

Her short laugh had an ugly sound. 'There's half a dozen 'breeds with the same idea, mister. They're working on rotgut booze. You ride over there now and you'll last as long as a snowball in hell. I told you Chepete's cronies don't like a white man.'

'All right, Toni. You're trying your damndest to scare me away from Chepete's place. Why?'

'I don't want to see you shot down, that's why,' she answered sullenly.

'If I had one guess coming,' Bryce's grin

twisted, 'I'd say you know where the money is hid. You got the information from Stephen before you stabbed him in the back with Gregory's Bowie knife.' Bryce watched her warily, ready to slap the gun from her hand if she pulled it.

'If I had another guess, I'd say you were coming back for it when the 'breeds finished their drunk and went home to sleep it off. That's how I got it figured, Toni.'

'I told you those 'breed cronies of Chepete's would be hunting for the booty from the stage hold-up.' Her eyes were half-lidded, crafty.

'Nobody but Chepete knew that Matthew and Stephen held up the stage, until you got Stephen to brag about it.' Bryce reached out suddenly and grabbed her wrist as her hand moved towards her gun. 'Chepete kept his mouth shut. So did you, Toni. There isn't a damn 'breed drunk or sober, man or woman, who knows about the hold-up money cache.'

Toni was breathing fast. She made no effort to free her wrist. 'Pick up the marbles, mister. I found the money in the hay and I've cached it where nobody but me can find it', she admitted. She leaned from her saddle and her lips brushed his. Bryce released her wrist.

'You're wrong about one guess, mister,' she said. 'When I leave here tonight, I'm travelling fast and I'm never coming back.' Her hand caressed the sack behind the high cantle of the saddle. 'I got my getaway stake here. If you'll come with me to Canada, a few months from now I'll tell you where I hid the stage money.'

'I told you I had a job to do here, Toni.'

'Quensel's Stranglers are waiting for you with a hangman's noose,' her voice was gritty, 'and it's not Quensel who gives the orders but Nile Carter. Nile has given orders to hang Sheriff Bryce Bradford if and when he brings in his prisoners and the loot. Does that change your mind about those chores you got in mind?'

Bryce shook his head. 'I got a letter signed by Nile Carter, warning me not to come back to Buffalo Run. What you just told me is old news, Toni.'

'What I'm telling you now,' the breed girl said, 'is older yet. It dates back to one Christmas Eve when Nile Carter was on the stagecoach that was held up by two masked road-agents. Three men were shot down in cold blood, but Nile Carter's life was spared. The next day she tried to buy a half-interest in the El Dorado.'

'What's wrong about that?' Bryce asked

with provocative calm.

'Nile Carter was broke,' Toni's voice was vibrant.

'How do you know how much money Nile had?'

'Because I saw all she had in her purse. It was noon and snowing when Jerry O'Toole drove to Chepete's for dinner and a change of horses. I talked a lot to Nile Carter that day. I wanted to be what she was, wearing beautiful clothes. When I told her that, she told me she was just an adventuress who made her money from cheating men. She opened her purse and showed me all the money she had to her name, but said that she had no intention of starving as long as there was a sucker left.

'But on Christmas Day she wanted to buy a half-interest in the El Dorado. What do you make of that?' Toni asked, but Bryce had no answer.

It all fitted into what Wade Applegate had told him last night as they sat and smoked and talked. Toni was repeating in her own words what the old man had told him. Nile Carter held a lot of hidden secrets locked somewhere inside.

Wade Applegate had told Bryce that Chepete knew a lot about the Christmas Eve stage hold-up. That he'd sell the information for a price. That if the play came up, Bryce could get the information from his daughter Toni, but to take care she didn't knife him in the back.

Bryce remembered the knife between Stephen's shoulder blades. When he looked at the half-breed girl, the black smoldering fire was back in her brooding eyes.

Bryce felt the cold knot that twisted his belly. 'The three men,' he kept his voice even toned, 'who were passengers on the stage. Did you talk to them?'

'No, I didn't. When I asked Nile about them she said one was a prisoner and the other two were guards, and that was all she knew. Why?'

'One of the men,' Bryce told her, 'the one who was a prisoner, was my father.'

'Oh.' The girl stared at him. 'He was killed, so you're tracking down the killers.'

'My father was murdered, shot down in cold blood. Nile Carter was there and saw it all,' Bryce forced a mirthless grin. 'That's another reason I'm taking the two dead men back to Buffalo Run. I want to have a talk with Nile Carter.'

'Are you in love with Nile?' Toni asked bluntly.

'What difference would that make?' Bryce said curtly.

'It would make a lot of difference,' Toni spoke with brutal frankness. 'If I were a man like you in love with a woman like Nile, I'd kill that tinhorn Quensel where I found him. You shot the wrong man when you killed Decker. He hated Nile Carter's guts.' She spoke vehemently.

'You shot Decker on account of Virginia Morgan,' Toni continued with a sneer. 'Don't tell me you're stuck on that high-toned little trick, mister.' Toni laughed, a short bitter laugh. 'Once again you shot the wrong man. It's Quensel who wants that little delicate magnolia bud from the south. He tossed Nile into the discard. That's how come Nile made a play for you.' Toni smiled thinly. 'It takes another female to figure out the treacherous tricks of the trade when another woman makes her move.'

Bryce's grin was twisted, bitter as the taste that came into his mouth. He had nothing to say.

They both heard the loud drunken shouts of the 'breeds on the other side of the creek.

Toni crowded her horse close. 'I've got to get gone,' she said. 'That drunken coyote pack are hunting for me right now. Help me get away, mister, and I'll tell you where I cached that money.' She reined her horse around.

'Head for Wade Applegate's ranch,' Bryce said as they rode away.

'I'm heading for the Canadian line,' Toni told him. 'For the Cypress Hills country.' She spurred her horse to a run and there was nothing for Bryce to do but follow.

After an hour's hard ride, they came to a deserted log cabin, well hidden in the brush. The girl reined up and swung to the ground, loosening the saddle cinch. Bryce dismounted and waited while Toni went into the cabin. He could hear her prowling around in the dark.

After a short while she came out into the moonlight, wiping dirt from a quart bottle of whisky on the front of her shirt. 'One of Chepete's crocks', she said. She pried the cork out and handed the bottle to Bryce.

'Ladies first,' Bryce grinned faintly.

'I'm no lady, mister,' Toni said bitterly. 'I'm a half-breed slut.' She lifted the bottle and drank a large swallow.

The front of her shirt was gaping open. Her faded overalls fitted skin-tight to the slim legs and around her lean flanks and small buttocks.

Back at the creek, in the red glow of the fire on the water, Toni had looked strangely beautiful in her red dress, in a wild pagan way that was clean and untouchable.

Now there was an unclean obscenity to her half revealed breasts, the tight fitting overalls. Her breath stank of whisky and her elfin face, with the large black eyes, the white teeth outlined by parted lips, and faintly swarthy skin, taut across high cheek bones, had changed to the cruel hard lines of her father's hatchet face. Her eyes were glinting slivers of black agate, cruel and cunning.

The soured stench of rotgut booze now mingled with the musky odor of her body. The look in Bryce's eyes must have revealed his thoughts because the girl turned away and walked over to sit on a fallen log.

'I lied about the money,' she said. 'That goat-whiskered old man was too foxy to bring more than a couple of hundred dollars to the Halfway House. I never saw the money and neither did Chepete. I lied to get you to come with me. But here is where our trails fork. You go your way. I'll go mine.'

'To hell with the money,' Bryce blundered. 'You think you can make it to the Canadian line from here alone?' he asked.

'Hell, yes. Quit crying about it.'

'Then you'd better get going,' Bryce tightened his saddle cinch. 'I'll hang around here for a while in case some 'breeds show up. It'll give you a head start.'

'You'll find the hold-up money buried in the dirt floor of this cabin, unless that cross-eyed Mormon lied with a knife twisted in his back.' Her laugh was short and nasty sounding. 'Take the money and the dead men to Buffalo Run. Maybe Nile Carter will pin a leather medal on you before she ties your rope necktie.'

Toni walked over to her horse and slowly tightened the saddle cinch. 'I figured if I got you this far,' she said without looking around. 'I could get you to go the rest of the way. We'd dig up the money and travel to hell and gone. Together.'

There was something in the tone of her voice and the way the 'breed girl said it, that kept Bryce tracked and without a word to say, until she had ridden out of sight.

He was unaware of the bottle in his hand until he started for the cabin. Then he threw it, smashing it against the log wall as he went in.

The dirt floor was hard packed. He went outside and prowled around till he found a broken shovel in under some brush.

He lit the stub of candle in the neck of a whisky bottle and started digging. Half an hour later he had the money dug up. He opened the canvas sack to make certain it was there before he tied it on behind his saddle cantle.

He headed back for Chepete's place with his Winchester carbine across his saddle in front of him. The first streaks of dawn were spreading the skyline when a lone rider came into sight. He came from the direction of the Halfway House.

The rider was Wade Applegate. Never had Bryce been so glad to see any man.

CHAPTER ELEVEN

The slow grin on the leathery face of Wade Applegate touched his eyes as he looked Bryce over from head to foot.

'It's good to see you, boy.' His quiet voice was vibrant. 'Good to see you alive.'

Bryce Bradford was strangely moved, touched deep by the older man's emotions. He nodded, too choked to trust his voice. Both men were trying to cover up any outward display of feelings as they dismounted.

'There was quite a gun ruckus at Chepete's place,' Bryce told the older man.

'I heard about it. When Big Gregory showed up with his girl, I saddled up and brought him back with me. Between us we managed to get the whole story from the older 'breeds and the women. I left Big Gregory there to swamp up. I picked up your trail. What happened to the 'breed girl?' Applegate asked.

Bryce untied the money sack. 'This is the money from the stage hold-up,' Bryce said. 'Toni took me to where Matthew and Stephen buried it at an old deserted log cabin. She told me where to dig, then she pulled out. Said she was heading for the Canadian line.'

'The girl got away with Chepete's money, so the 'breeds say.'

'I know. Toni said she was claiming it, that she'd earned every dollar of it,' Bryce said defensively.

'She has every right to the money,' Wade Applegate said. 'She hid her sister in the dug-out celler, put on her red dress and substituted her body for Marie's.'

'I don't know how Toni got hold of the money. Last time I saw the sack of money, Chepete was hugging it against his gunshot belly,' Bryce said.

'Chepete's squaw took it into their cabin when she dragged her dead husband in,' Applegate told Bryce. 'Toni slipped in by the back door, changed from the red dress to overalls and shirt. She had a cartridge belt buckled on and a gun in her hand, ready to shoot down anybody who got in her way. She took the money sack with her. Marie found her squaw mother lying on the bed. She was dead.' Wade Applegate said grimly.

'You think Toni killed her own mother?' Bryce asked.

'It was the squaw's skinning knife that

killed her. She wanted to give the money to Marie because she was like her in every respect, even-tempered, dull-witted. She hated Toni because she took after Chepete. I figure that when Toni took the money, the squaw tried to stab her.'

'She's a wildcat', Bryce said. 'She wanted me to go along with her. I still don't feel right about letting her ride off alone.'

'Forget the 'breed girl Chepete trained to steal and cheat and kill.' Wade Applegate looked at Bryce. 'Toni is plenty capable of taking care of herself and she'd have knifed you like she put a knife between Stephen's shoulder blades and did the same to her own mother after they'd fought over the money.'

They left it like that. But the half-breed girl and the memory of her would never be forgotten by Bryce Bradford.

Bryce handed the money sack to Wade Applegate, who tied it on his saddle. Then both men squatted on their boot heels facing one another.

'I'm taking the dead bodies of Matthew and Stephen to Buffalo Run', Bryce told Applegate.

'The 'breeds threw the two bodies into the burning building,' Applegate told him.

'The fire cremated those two Avenging Angels.'

'Saves me that trouble, then', said Bryce. 'But I'm headed for Buffalo Run anyway. I found out a few things at the Halfway House that ties in with that other Christmas Eve stage hold-up.' Bryce told Wade Applegate everything that Toni had told him.

The older man filled his pipe and put it in a corner of his mouth. 'Have you figured out your method of approach when you get there?' he asked.

'Only that I'm going to get the truth out of Nile Carter and Quensel.'

'Don't forget the stagedriver, Jerry O'Toole, also Big Tim Fogarty and Pete Kaster. They know plenty.'

'I want to find out who killed my father,' Bryce said. 'And what happened to the tithe money he had in the black satchel. Also if Nile Carter was in cahoots with the two road-agents.'

'That's a big sized order for one man to handle.'

'It's strictly a one man job,' Bryce replied.

'How about your sheriff's job? Are you going to use your legal authority to back any play you make?' asked Wade Applegate.

Bryce Bradford's laugh had an ugly sound. 'When I locate the two men who murdered my father, I'll kill them where I find them. Regardless.'

They were silent for a while, then Bryce said, 'I was sent out to catch the road-agents and bring them back, dead or alive, together with the loot.' Bryce smiled thinly. 'I'm going back empty-handed.'

'They'll be waiting with a hangman's rope for you, Bryce, so watch yourself,' the old rancher warned. His pipe had gone out. He knocked the cold ashes into the palm of his hand and blew them down wind.

'I figure Jerry O'Toole, the stagedriver,' he said, 'knows who held up the stage that Christmas Eve. I was in town when he drove in. Nile Carter was on the driver's seat beside him. That old rascal has a roving eye for the ladies and he was drunker than usual. A girl of Nile's calibre could twist Jerry around her little finger. If he knew who the road-agents were it's a cinch bet that she shared his secret by the time they reached Buffalo Run.'

'I sure played into her hands when I killed Charlie Decker,' Bryce grinned ruefully. 'She claimed Decker's share in the El Dorado. Made me a proposition to kill Quensel and become her partner.'

'You turned her down?'

'I told her I was drifting on.' Bryce took Nile's note from his pocket and handed it to the older man.

Wade Applegate read the note that warned Bryce never to return to Buffalo Run, and that Morgan and his daughter had left for Fort Benton.

'How does it add up in your tally book, Bryce?' asked Wade Applegate, returning the note to Bryce.

'A Strangler's necktie party when I get there,' Bryce answered with a twisted grin. He remembered the half-breed girl's words; 'Nile might pin a leather medal on you before she ties your rope necktie.'

'Did it ever occur to you that Nile Carter's life might be in grave danger?' Wade Applegate's question drove the remembered thoughts from Bryce's mind.

'Nile Carter probably had a reason for sending you that note of warning,' Applegate said. He walked to his horse and swung into the saddle, then said, 'I'm riding to Buffalo Run with you.'

Bryce mounted and together the two men rode side by side into the dawn, its leaden grey sky streaked with crimson that looked like fresh blood on a dirty grey blanket.

CHAPTER TWELVE

It was somewhere around midnight when Bryce Bradford and Wade Applegate reached the little cowtown of Buffalo Run.

They had decided to stop at Nile Carter's house at the edge of town first. Lamplight showed behind closely pulled blinds in the living-room and bedroom and in the kitchen.

They rode around back. Wade Applegate told Bryce to stay in the saddle as he dismounted and handed him his bridle reins.

Bryce had an uneasy feeling as he watched the squawman stop at the kitchen door and rap. He was unarmed.

The kitchen door opened a crack and the moon-faced squaw peered out. The squawman spoke softly in the Sioux language and the door opened wide enough to let him in.

Bryce waited impatiently, his nerves taut. It seemed a long time before the squawman came out, carrying a bag. 'Do you recognize this?' he asked holding it up to Bryce.

Bryce took the satchel from him and

after examining it, he said, 'It belonged to my father. He kept his tithe money in it.'

'Nile Carter told the squaw to give it to you when you showed up. The money has never been touched. She left a message for you to take it and hit the trail back to wherever you came from.'

Bryce Bradford's lips skinned back in a sneering grin as he wedged the satchel between his belly and the saddlehorn. 'Anything else?' he asked, his bloodshot eyes splinters of steel.

'There's to be a wedding here at midnight,' Applegate said. 'I got a glimpse of the bride waiting alone in a big armchair. It's Virginia Morgan and she's going to be married to Jack Quensel.'

Bryce started to get off his horse, but Wade Applegate put an arm out to hold him in the saddle. 'No use you blundering in there. The squaw told me Quensel had sold out to Nile Carter and that he and his bride were quitting Montana, never to return. He's taking Virginia to New Orleans to live.'

Bryce Bradford sat wedged in his saddle. His heavy brows knit in a scowl as he forced clarity of thought through his confused, bewildered brain.

He and Wade Applegate had made a

long, hard ride to Buffalo Run, to save Nile Carter from threatened danger. Now Nile was in power here. She and Quensel had made some kind of a deal. It was Virginia Morgan who was in danger and in need of help. It looked as if her drunken father had sold his daughter down the river.

If Nile Carter had a notion she could buy him off, scare him out of the country, she had the wrong man.

'I'm going on to the El Dorado,' Bryce's voice was deadly quiet.

'You could be walking into a gun trap, Bryce. Set by Quensel and baited with two women.'

A few minutes later they rode into the wide doorway of the barn to stable the horses that had packed them a long way. They swung to the ground.

'Good Gawdamighty!' Old Dad Jones's whisky voice came from the dark shadows of the barn. 'It's Bryce Bradford come back, and Wade Applegate with him. Time you got the snakes out of your boots, Jerry.'

The grizzled barnman and the tipsy stagedriver came out of the barn. Bryce took the black satchel from his saddle and waited until the two cronies came close before he spoke.

'Who were the two road-agents who held up your stage on Christmas Eve a year ago?' Bryce looked straight at Jerry O'Toole and waited for his answer.

The half-drunk stagedriver recoiled a step. 'Fer the love of Judas, how could I tell who was behind a black handkerchief mask?' he whined.

The squawman took a quick step forward. His strong, gnarled hands fastened on the collar of his flannel shirt, twisting it tight as a rope around O'Toole's neck.

'Love of Judas!' Jerry's eyes rolled towards Dad Jones. 'Are you goin' to stand there, begobs, like a dumb bastid and let this squawman choke me black in the face? Lend a hand.'

'Tell the man, Jerry.' Old Dad spat tobacco juice on the floor. 'Get it off your mind. Hell, you ain't gone to confession since you was an altar boy in County Cork. Do you good. Like a dose of caster oil.' The barnman winked at Wade Applegate.

'They'll hang me,' wailed the terrified stagedriver.

'I'm choking you down right now,' said Wade Applegate, putting pressure on the twist of the shirt collar.

'It was Charlie Decker,' grasped Jerry O'Toole. 'Decker and Quensel.'

Wade Applegate cut a look at Bryce as he slowly loosened his twisting grip.

'Where did Nile Carter fit into the deal?' demanded Bryce. 'Was she in cahoots with Decker and Quensel?'

'Hell, no,' Jerry snorted. 'And that I'll swear to. Decker shot the two younger men and Quensel shot the older man when he reached for a gun. Nile Carter witnessed the killings and Decker wanted to kill her, but Quensel drawed the line at killing a woman. Especially a colleen as purty as that one.'

'Go easy!' Dad Jones's whisky breath blew hot in Bryce's face as he stood close. 'Quensel's expecting you back tonight. I was to keep you here till Jerry had time to get to the El Dorado to say that you had arrived.'

'I'm much obliged to you, Dad,' Bryce told him.

Jerry O'Toole's bleared eyes bugged out when he saw the black satchel. 'That satchel belonged to the older man Quensel shot', he volunteered.

'Go on. Who got the satchel?' Bryce snapped.

'Nile Carter had it when she rode with me on the driver's seat. I handed it down to her when we reached Buffalo Run,' he said.

The two men unsaddled. Wade Applegate took the money sack from his saddle. The barnman and the stagedriver led the two horses into a double stall and piled hay in the manger, giving each horse a gallon of grain.

Bryce and Applegate stood there wordless, each thinking their own thoughts, the black satchel and the canvas sack at their feet on the floor of the barn.

Bryce's eyes narrowed when he saw the big brown gelding in the Square and Compass brand in the first stall. 'That's the horse the 'breed girl made her getaway on,' he told the squawman, puzzlement in his eyes.

Old Dad Jones said quickly, 'One of Chepete's girls stabled the horse. The wild one, Toni. She told me it was money she had in the bloody-looking sack she carried across the shoulder of her red shirt. Said she was going to buck the tiger at the El Dorado, show Nile Carter the difference between foolin' around and playin' for keeps. Last I seen, she was headed that way. She had a six-shooter buckled on.'

Wade Applegate picked up the money sack and reached for the black satchel. 'I'll take the satchel,' he told Bryce, 'to balance the load. You might need both hands.'

'There'll be a Hot Time in the Old Town Tonight,' Old Dad piped up, a little off-key.

CHAPTER THIRTEEN

Bryce Bradford and Wade Applegate peered through the windows of the El Dorado. Tobacco smoke hung in thick layers and blobs of yellow light showed foggily from the half dozen big nickled Rochester lamps that hung by chains high above the heads of the milling crowd lined up at the long bar and clustered around the gambling layouts.

The orchestra pit below the level of the stage was empty. The keys of the upright piano were covered. No kerosene lights burned in the row of floodlights. The red drapes of the half dozen boxes on either side of the barn-like vast room were pulled back, except the front box above the stage. The curtains on it were pulled together. It was the private box where Nile Carter had taken Bryce Bradford on the first night in the cow town.

At the far end of the room the packed crowd was standing motionless, backed up a dozen deep behind a roped-in enclosure. Inside the heavy rawhide rope corral was a big roulette wheel, and spinning the wheel was Nile Carter. The high stool behind her, where the lookout usually sat, was empty.

Nile wore a sleeveless, low-cut evening gown of charcoal black satin. Her tawny hair was plaited in heavy braids and coiled around her head like a crown of burnished gold. Even through the smoke haze, her amber eyes glinted. A bitter, contemptuous smile twisted her red lips as her long, shapely, ringless fingers spun the wheel.

Toni, the half-breed girl, was the only player inside the roped-in enclosure. Her high crowned dusty black hat was on the floor behind her, half covering the canvas money sack. Her black hair hung down her back in two squaw braids. Her scarlet silk shirt was open at the throat. The blood had drained from her face and her black eyes glowed like smoldering red coals in the smoky lamplight. Red lips were peeled back to show her white teeth as she reached both hands into the almost empty sack to scoop out a double handful of crumpled bank notes and gold coins.

Toni dumped the pile on the table, bunching it together in a tight wad over the color red. She played only the red numbers, disregarding the others.

The spinning wheel slowed down. The little ivory ball bounced a few times and fell into a slot and stayed there, the white ball showing against the black.

Nile hooked in the pile of money with an ebony handled rake.

The half-breed girl upended the canvas sack on the table.

Jack Quensel was nowhere in sight. Judge Plato Morgan stood alone at the far end of the bar, a half-filled bottle of whisky and a pitcher of cracked ice in front of him. He held a filled glass in his hand as he stared into space with unseeing eyes. There was something tragic about the black clad erect figure in the black Confederate hat.

Big Tim Fogarty and Pete Kaster stood together at the bar. Both looked freshly barbered and were dressed in their best clothes. They held drinks in their hands and each had a whisky bottle in front of him. They watched the crowd with shifting, restless, wary eyes.

The hands of the big clock over the back bar showed the hour to be thirty minutes past eleven o'clock.

Nile spun the wheel, sending the ivory ball in the opposite direction. A hush fell like a smoke pall while the white ball dropped into a black slot.

Two pairs of eyes, one greenish-yellow,

the other red-black fire met and held across the wheel.

'Red for blood,' the almost whispered words hissed from behind Toni's bared teeth. 'Black for death.' The Colt pistol in her hand was pointed at Nile's breast.

Nile used both hands to shove the big pile of money slowly towards the half-breed girl. 'The wheel's fixed for suckers', she said in a voice as cold as the glint in her eyes. 'Put the money in your bloody sack. Then get out. Don't come back Injun.'

Nile turned her back on the gun in the 'breed girl's tense hand. The crowd parted as she crossed the floor towards the stage and disappeared inside the curtained box above.

Toni reached for the empty sack. Holding it open below the level of the table she used the long barrel of the six-shooter to scrape the money into it. She pulled the string to close the bag and picked up her hat, slanting it on her head. Her jaws were clamped till the muscles bunched and quivered, her lips pulled taut. A thin, greyish film hooded the black eyes as she slung the sack over her shoulder. Every man in the place was watching her as she crossed the floor, the gun in her hand.

Toni opened the door to the back alley and went out without a backward glance.

The tense-packed crowd slowly relaxed. The shuffling of booted feet mingled with men's voices that were low toned, hushed.

'Stay here, Wade,' Bryce said. 'I'm going to find Quensel.' His hand was on his gun as he shouldered through the swinging half-doors, leaving the older man alone outside.

Fogarty and Kaster sighted Bryce the second he came in. They stiffened, exchanging quick meaning glances. Neither man made a move towards a gun as Bryce stopped just beyond the long reach of Big Tim.

'Where is Jack Quensel hiding out?' Bryce put the question to both men, the tone of his voice deadly.

The two men moved apart as if to make room for Bryce at the bar.

'By Gawdamighty,' Fogarty mumbled and belched into Bryce's face, 'that's what me'n Pete are beginning to wonder. Belly up to the mahogany, Sheriff. Have a drink.'

'Where's Quensel?' Bryce repeated, ignoring the invitation to drink.

Bryce had seen the quick exchange of glances, the slight shift of Pete Kaster's shoulder and arm. He ducked his head with a quick jerk as Kaster threw the contents of his whisky glass into his face. Bryce's hat caught the splash of whisky.

Bryce moved in swiftly, covering the scant three feet distance in one quick jump that slammed him into Kaster. The short, burly man was thrown off-balance by the hard impact as he slid a .45 from its holster.

Bryce grabbed the thick wrist as Kaster thumbed back the gun hammer. He jerked the wrist downward in a twist that put the muzzle deep in Kaster's paunch just as Kaster squeezed the trigger. The soft-nosed bullet ripped through the hard layers of fat into the man's belly, tearing a ragged hole at the base of his spine.

The bared grin was frozen on Tim Fogarty's red jowled face. His heavy, ham-like fist clenched around the thick shot glass as he swung a wild haymaker at Bryce's head. Bryce threw the gutshot Pete Kaster at Fogarty and the big man's fist crashed into the twisted face of the dying man before he could pull the punch.

Bryce moved in and the barrel of his gun chopped down behind Tim Fogarty's ear. It was short and savage enough to make Fogarty's knees buckle, and he pitched headlong across the body of his side-partner who lay sprawled against the brass foot rail.

Bryce backed away, his gun ready. He was half-crouched, feet balanced to twist or jump in any direction, his eyes slivered, dangerous. He was set and ready to shoot. The packed crowd of men stood frozen, held by the levelled gun, the killer's look in Bryce's eyes.

Without turning his head, Bryce was aware of Wade Applegate standing near him.

Bryce looked up over the heads of the silent crowd. Nile Carter had parted the drapes, to stand there in her black satin sheath, her pale amber eyes fixed on him, a cold smile on her lips.

The creak of a pulley squealed like a rat. The stage curtain raised slowly, pulled by unseen hands back stage. Men twisted their heads, shuffling their booted feet around. An almost inaudible mutter swept the crowd, like a dry, invisible fox-fire.

There on the stage was a wooden gallows, its thirteen steps leading to a high platform, a hangman's rope hung down from the ridge-log. You could tell by the surprised hush that gripped the men, that they were seeing the gruesome stage setting for the first time.

Bryce cut a quick look upward. His eyes met Nile's fixed stare. Then her hand beckoned him. The drapes fell back into place.

Big Tim Fogarty raised himself from the floor. His big hands reached up to the edge of the bar and pull himself up. Blood from a torn ear trickled down to stain his starched shirt bosom. His eyes found Bryce Bradford and a wide grin spread across his face.

'I warned Quensel,' the big man's chuckle came from deep inside him, 'that he had a grizzly by the tail.' He reached behind him and grabbed a whisky bottle by the neck. He smashed the end on the edge of the bar.

'Any you sonabitches want the sheriff, start movin'! You gotta pass me to get to him.' He waved the jagged bottle in a sweeping gesture. 'Them as don't want Bryce Bradford hung, belly up to the bar.'

The crowd moved as one man towards the bar.

Bryce shoved his gun into its holster. There was a grim set to his jaw as he took the satchel from the older man's hand.

'You saw her,' Bryce said in a tight voice. 'I'm going up there.'

'You could be walking into a death trap,'

Wade Applegate told him.

'It won't be the first time,' Bryce said.

'I'll be having a drink at the bar,' the older man said. 'I'll keep my eye peeled for any trouble up there.'

CHAPTER FOURTEEN

Bryce Bradford carried the black satchel in his left hand, to keep his gun hand free, as he went up the enclosed stairway and along a narrow passageway to the last box.

He parted the drapes with the pistol barrel and peered inside. Nile Carter was the sole occupant. She was sitting at a small table, an iced bucket of champagne on the floor beside her chair, and two champagne glasses on the table.

Bryce stepped into the box and put the satchel on the table. Nile looked at him across the table, then said softly, 'The man who owned that bag was shot down in cold blooded murder. I saw it happen.'

'That man was my father,' Bryce tried to keep emotion from his voice.

'I found that out after you were gone,' Nile said. 'That is why I did everything I knew to keep you from coming back here.'

'Even to marrying off Virginia Morgan to the killer who shot my father,' Bryce retorted bitterly.

'Not that.' Her cold smile tightened her lips. 'Quensel arranged that. I don't know what threats he used by way of persuasion.'

'Who arranged the stage setting below?' Bryce sneered.

'Quensel's men moved it in, while he and I were drawing up the sale papers for the El Dorado at my cottage. Quensel's price was the black satchel of money. The payoff was to be at midnight tonight. He gave his gambler's word he'd leave Buffalo Run tonight and quit Montana for good.

'Then when I returned to the El Dorado, that half-breed girl came in. She said she had enough money in the sack over her shoulder to buy the El Dorado, lock, stock and barrel. She insisted on gambling me for the place. Either I'd gamble or she'd kill me. She had a gun in her hand and meant business. She wanted to buck the wheel, play the red. She kept looking at the dress I have on, saying, "Red for blood. Black for death." I don't scare easily but the look in her black eyes had cold shivers running down my spine.'

'I know what you mean,' Bryce said grimly. 'I want to know everything you can tell me about my father's murder, Nile.'

'Decker and Quensel held up the stagecoach. It was Quensel who shot your father. I could have told you that the first night we met, but you never asked me.'

'I didn't know about it until the half-breed girl told me about the Christmas Eve hold-up.' His eyes narrowed. 'Were you in on it?' he asked.

'No. I never saw Quensel or Decker until that Christmas Eve.' Nile reached for the satchel. 'I've never tampered with the lock on this bag. You can see that the lead your father poured into the locking mechanism has never been broken. I live on the money I make dealing cards.'

Bryce bent over to examine the lock and verify her statement.

'I used that satchel to blackmail Quensel,' she admitted. 'I used it tonight to drive Quensel out of Montana.'

'Why?' Bryce asked.

'I got word that Bryce Bradford was coming back to Buffalo Run. I didn't want Quensel to kill you.'

'Where is Quensel?'

'He dropped from sight a few hours ago. The last I saw of him was when he left my cottage with the agreement we'd made up, which was to be signed when I laid the satchel of money on the line at midnight.' Nile looked at her watch. 'It's fifteen minutes till midnight. Quensel's wedding and the pay-off is set for that hour, his favorite time to do business.'

'There'll be one uninvited guest at Quensel's wedding,' Bryce said.

'How do you know that Quensel is not expecting you?' Nile stood up, reaching for the champagne bottle. There was a card wired to its neck. She held it out for Bryce to read.

'For Nile Carter and Bryce Bradford; to drink a toast to Jack Quensel and Virginia Morgan on their wedding night.'

'It was here when I finished spinning the wheel for the half-breed girl and came up to the box.' Nile smiled faintly.

Bryce put his hand on the satchel. 'You were going to double-cross Quensel on the pay-off.' It was a flat statement but there was a puzzled question in it.

'There was an element of chance,' Nile smiled enigmatically. 'Both of us were aware of it. Both of us high stake gamblers playing a cut-throat game. Neither of us knows how much money is in the satchel. It could be filled with rocks.

'That black satchel has become a symbol, an evil, deadly symbol. Tainted with the crime of murder and the more insidious evil of a blackmail threat. Quensel was buying my silence.'

'Honor among thieves,' Bryce said brutally.

'Ouch!' Nile smiled. 'I asked for that one.'

'You two gamblers don't trust one another', Bryce said. 'While Quensel made secret plans to marry Virginia Morgan, using some kind of threat to put the squeeze on the Morgans, you made secret plans to turn the satchel over to me when I showed up. Thank God I'm no gambler,' Bryce said contemptuously.

'Your return was a gamble,' Nile told him. 'When you came in here with the satchel, you took chips in the game.'

Bryce laughed shortly. 'You used the satchel as a threat against Quensel. You used it to buy me off, leaving word with your squaw housekeeper for me to run away from Quensel and the Stranglers of Buffalo Run.' His voice was tense with anger. 'You were out to save Nile Carter!'

Her amber eyes looked at him for a long moment, studying him, probing deep into his mixed emotions. Whatever she found there brought a faint smile to her lips.

'I've been taking Nile Carter's part for a long time. When a woman has the guts to battle for existence, she uses her sex as the deadliest weapon of all. Whatever I've done, I was out to save the body of Nile Carter, regardless, and to hell with her soul.' Her voice was vibrant.

Leaving Quensel's card wired to the bottle neck, she lifted the champagne from the bucket of ice and began twisting the cork. It popped like a pistol shot.

The drapes stirred gently. Wade Applegate stepped into the box, alarm in his eyes. He still had the sack of money in his hand.

'Forgive the intrusion', he said. 'I was waiting for Bryce in the passageway when I heard what sounded like a shot.'

There was a mocking smile on Nile's lips and a challenge in her eyes as she handed each man a filled glass of champagne. Then she took a third glass from a shelf in the corner of the booth and poured herself a drink.

'To whatever the future may hold,' she said as they raised glasses and drank. Her voice was level toned as she looked at both men.

Bryce felt the sharp, cold, needle-like sparking wine as it went down his throat, quenching the parched thirst within him, cooling his temper and heated blood.

'The chips are down,' Wade Applegate said as he set the empty glass on the table. 'Within the hour the game will be over.'

Nile twisted the hollow stem of her emptied glass. Her eyes flicked the sack of money in Applegate's hand. 'What's that?' she asked.

'Tithe money,' he told her. 'It was collected from Quensel by two Avenging Angels sent out by the outcast Mormons of Rainbow's End. It's the money Quensel was expecting on the stage that was held up.'

A dark shadow crossed Wade Applegate's eyes as they looked inward. He said slowly, 'The two Avenging Angels are dead. There will be no more sent out from Rainbow's End. Bryce does not belong to the Mormon Church, therefore, he owes no tithe. His father's tithe in the black satchel has been cancelled out by the hand of God. The money now belongs to the boy.'

'What becomes of the money you have there, Mr. Applegate?' Nile asked.

'This money belongs to me,' he said, holding the sack up. 'I'll try to explain it. Decker and Quensel robbed the stage on Christmas Eve a year ago and got away with seventy-five thousand dollars I had consigned to the Bank at Fort Benton. The sixty thousand in this sack belonging to Quensel was lifted by those two Avenging Angels and recovered by Bryce. I'm claiming it from Quensel to repay part of the money he stole from me.' The eyes of the white-haired man were cold as winter ice as he looked at Nile Carter.

Nile Carter's amber eyes paled. She reached into the low-cut neckline of her dress and now held a snub-barrelled .38 belly gun in her hand. 'Get the hell out of town, both of you.' The gun was levelled at Applegate's waistline.

'When I've killed Quensel,' Bryce spoke tensely, 'I'll be glad to leave Buffalo Run. But not until then.'

'You both saw the gallows set up on the stage below. If I were to give the word, those Stranglers down there would hang you both.' Nile's mouth flattened into a thin, lipless slit. 'Tell the damned fool to get away, Applegate, or I'll kill you where you stand.'

The squawman's blue eyes were cold, calculating. 'Which one of the two men, Bryce or Quensel, are you trying to save?' he asked quietly.

'What difference does it make?' Nile's voice had a scratchy sound.

'Decker wanted to kill you when the stage was held up', Wade Applegate said, ignoring her question. 'You owe your life to Quensel.' He paid no attention to the

186

gun in her hand. 'It's a shame to let that vintage wine go wasted', he said, a slow grin on his mouth.

'Damn you, Wade Applegate,' Nile's voice broke like a shattered wine glass. She slid the gun into the front of her dress and looked at her watch.

'Ten minutes till midnight,' she told them. She splashed champagne into the glasses. 'The hour set for Quensel's wedding, and Nile Carter's wedding gift.' She nudged the satchel with the bottle, then dropped it into the bucket.

Nile Carter stood facing the two men, the blood drained from her face, a film of unshed tears in her eyes, her lower lip caught and held between her teeth, bitten down until a drop of blood showed.

None of them saw the half-breed girl standing just inside the drapes. Her moccasined feet had made no sound. Her heavy hair had come unbraided and fresh wet blood streaked her pale face. Her red shirt was sodden with sticky blood that oozed sluggishly from a bullet rip across her collar-bone. She clung with one hand to the drapes, holding the .45 in the other blood-smeared hand. The croaking sound she made whirled Bryce around.

He made a dive for the gun as Toni let

go the curtain to lift the gun with both hands. The gun was pointed at Nile. Bryce grabbed the barrel and twisted it upward just as it exploded.

Bryce caught the girl as she swayed and pitched headlong into his arms. Her eyes were pain-seared in the dim lamplight. He eased her to the floor and knelt on one knee. 'Who shot you, Toni?' he asked gently.

'Quensel. Nile Carter's tinhorn. He's drunk,' Toni whispered.

Nile knelt beside the girl. She soaked the towel around the champagne bottle in the ice water and laid it across the bullet wound.

'Tell us what happened, Toni,' Bryce said.

'Judge Morgan bumped into me as I went out into the alley. He asked me to help him get Virginia away from Nile's house. The squaw and I sneaked her out the back door. She acted like she didn't know where she was or that we were taking her away. We hid her out in the squaw camp across the creek. The squaw stayed with her. I went back to the house where Judge Morgan was.'

Bryce held the champagne bottle to Toni's mouth and let her swallow. She forced a smile. 'Bottle-raised on Chepete's rotgut. Never got weaned.' She pulled the bottle away to talk again.

'Quensel was in the house, drunk as a 'breed fiddler. The old judge went after him with a sword cane. Quensel shot the judge, then grabbed me before I could get away. I clawed loose and ran. He took a couple of pot shots at me, but I kept on going. I was after Nile. She'd put me on the Injun list.' Toni took another swallow.

'Quensel's out to kill you, Bryce. I had to find you to tell you before I died. You're a hell of a good man, Bryce.'

'You're not going to die, Toni,' Bryce tried to make it sound convincing.

'The hell I ain't. I'm a no-good half-breed slut.'

Nile took the wet towel and rinsed it in the ice water and wiped the blood from the girl's face. 'You're a half-breed, Toni, but you're no slut. You got more guts than any female I ever met.' Nile smiled at her, and asked, 'You still got that sack of money, Toni?'

Toni nodded, but her eyes narrowed with suspicion.

'You'll need it for a bank-roll to run the El Dorado. I'm giving you the place. I'll put it in writing,' Nile told her.

'I tried to kill you', Toni said.

'I humiliated you. So you took a shot at me. That crosses it off the books. You now own the El Dorado, but don't try to thank me. I hate the place. I was going to set fire to it at midnight tonight.'

The half-breed girl lay back. The champagne had brought the natural colour back into her face and red-lipped smile. The black fire smouldered in her eyes as she realized the fulfilment of her dream of owning a place like the El Dorado.

'I'll change the name,' she whispered. 'Toni's Place, in big red letters. I'll wear a black dress like yours.'

Toni reached up and pulled Bryce's face down to hers and fastened her red lips on his mouth in a bruising kiss. Then her lips slid away and her head fell back.

'Quensel,' she told him, 'is at the squaw camp in the tepee where we took Virginia Morgan. He's drunk and wrapped up in an Injun blanket with his bride.' Toni's laugh pierced his eardrum as she raised her head to his. 'You did me a favor, remember? I pay my debts, good and bad. I set Quensel up for you, easy as shooting a duck on a pond, Bryce.'

The 'breed girl's laugh was like the scratch of a broken needle across a dark window-pane. Her fingers, sticky with fresh blood, fastened into Bryce's hair as she held his head down against hers.

'I hid the sack of money under a buffalo robe in the bride's tepee. Fetch it back to me when you kill Quensel.' Her mouth fastened on his again, then she lay back, a bitter, twisted smile on her mouth, the black fire dying out of her eyes. 'Good huntin', Bryce,' were her last words.

Chepete's half-breed daughter had died dreaming, all debts paid off according to her lights.

Nile covered Toni's face with a thin black scarf that had covered her bare shoulders. She turned to face Bryce Bradford. 'Before you go, Bryce,' her voice was barely audible, 'I want you to know this. Nile Carter has never given herself to any man on earth.' She put both hands on his shoulders, holding him away, and said, 'I'll be waiting for you Bryce.'

Bryce pulled Nile into his arms. The sob she had been holding back found release as her parted lips met his. Bryce felt the long shudder of her body as it pressed close against him in a woman's complete surrender. There was no need for spoken words during those long, lingering moments of parting. Perhaps it was to be a final parting. Both were aware of that dread thought as Nile's arms tightened, holding him there in a final, desperate effort.

Never had life seemed more precious to Bryce Bradford. He had found everything he had ever dreamed of as he held Nile Carter in close embrace. He was too young to die, too filled with the zest for living now to be shot down.

It took a lot of will power for Bryce to pull himself away. He looked around dazedly. Wade Applegate was no longer there.

Nile looked at her watch. It was five minutes till midnight.

'Toni's gun is gone,' Bryce spoke in a harsh whisper. 'Wade Applegate took it along.'

'What's wrong with that, Bryce?'

'He never owned a gun, never shot a gun in his life. It was a part of his religion. He's doing this on my account. I'm not going to let him. It's my job to kill the man who murdered my father.'

Bryce's eyes were slivered, bleak, as he pulled the drapes aside and strode out of the box, running blindly. 'Stay here, Nile,' he called as he ran. 'Wait there till I come back for you.'

CHAPTER FIFTEEN

Pale moonlight flooded the hundred yards of clearing. Beyond it showed the white picket fence and the whitewashed log cottage that belonged to Nile Carter. Lamplight showed from every window.

Bryce was well aware of the desperate chance he would have to take to cross the clearing. There was no sign of movement around the house but there could be hidden guns in the lilac hedge that laned the walk.

There was only one way to play it, to Bryce's way of thinking. That was to walk out into the open as if he feared nothing and no man this side of hell. Take his time. Don't run like he was scared of being shot down. On the other hand, don't drag his feet like he was forcing himself to face something that chilled his guts.

The trick was to step out like he was asking for a showdown. Like he didn't give a damn, win or draw. If Quensel were bushed up, watching, let the tinhorn get a good look at a man who had the guts to come out in the open. If he lacked the courage to fight out in the open, let him do his bushwhacking, and to hell with it.

Bryce was checking it to Quensel. If he was the high stake gambler he claimed to be, let him prove it. Bryce kept telling himself that with every step he took. But he didn't believe any part of it.

Quensel was a cold-blooded killer. He did his gambling with a cold deck, the cards marked and the odds always in his favor. Quensel never gave a sucker a break, and Bryce Bradford was a sucker, every step he took.

Quensel had shot Bryce's father down in cold blood. Tonight he had shot the white-maned Judge Morgan. He had shot the half-breed girl. Quensel would never give a man like Bryce an even chance. Amen to that.

Bryce told himself that he was whistling in the dark. A stiff-lipped grin forced its way across his face. He reached for the gate, clicked it open and walked down the gravel path. The tall lilac hedge on either side cast dark shadows in front of him. Bryce slid his gun out and gripped it in a moist palm, but nothing moved and no sound broke the hushed quiet.

Bryce stepped up on the vine-covered porch. When he was sure no one was hiding there, he peered into the living-room window. Through the lace curtains he saw the body of Judge Plato Morgan lying sprawled, face down, on the carpeted floor, his cane gripped in his dead hand. The fringe of his thick white hair was tipped in the puddle of blood that stained the carpet.

There was no sign of Wade Applegate or Big Tim Fogarty, or the man Bryce had come to kill. But Nile's squaw housekeeper was in the kitchen, a sawed-off scatter gun, across her wide lap. Bryce felt the full impact of her stare as he entered by the back door.

'Quensel is in the tepee with his woman,' she said when she recognized Bryce, speaking in a guttural voice that was startling. 'That white man crazy. You kill him. You go to tepee, cross the bridge. Quick as hell!'

Bryce lost no time. He was across the bridge and following a dim twisting trail through the brush that hid his cautious movements. He saw the high lodge poles of a tepee ahead along a creek bank. The tepee flap was propped half open, held in place by a long stick.

Bryce shifted his gun to his left hand and wiped the sweat from the palm of his gun hand along the seat of his britches. He could see shadowy movements inside the dark tepee, then he heard the flat sound of Quensel's voice.

'. . . you appeared like a frail, beautiful ghost that came out of a dead past to haunt me. You rose from the grave of a girl I once loved. A girl of delicate beauty, with hair like pale moonbeams spun on a golden spinning-wheel by the hands of angels.' A short laugh that had a bitter metallic sound came from inside the tepee, then the voice went on.

'. . . the same pale translucent skin as yours that comes from generations of line breeding, to keep the same blue blood of the first families of Virginia untainted. . . .' The voice broke off. A cork twisted from a bottle.

'I was a beardless young Captain of the Confederate Cavalry then but not good enough for a Virginia blueblood. When she refused my offer of marriage, insane with jealousy and hurt pride, I organized Quensel's Guerrilla Raiders and we did some plundering, raping and burning before I lost interest and came west.' The laugh sounded again, the laugh of a man gone insane. 'I turned her over to my raiders to rape and murder. I killed her

father, her brother who'd been my class mate. I set fire to the colonial mansion.'
An empty bottle was flung out of the tepee, crashing against a rock. A string of foul blasphemy spilled out and again that crazy laugh.

'I left my true identity in the south. I chose the name of Quensel from a tomb-stone in a New Orleans graveyard. I dis-banded my guerrillas after I'd sobered up from a long debauchery with John Barley-corn. I had regained some of my sanity when I reached Buffalo Run. Then you came out of the past. . . .' Quensel laughed again. Then lurched out of the tepee.

He stood in the moonlight on wide-spread legs, his eyes burning in a greyish twisted mask of insane hatred. His hand gripped a gun.

Bryce Bradford stepped out into the moonlight, his gun-barrel tilted, ready to level down and fire. They faced one an-other across a fifty foot distance, their eyes held gripped for a long moment.

'When I count three,' a calm voice spoke from the footbridge, 'shoot at will.'

Wade Applegate stood on the bridge, bareheaded, the moonlight on his shock of white hair. Tall, erect, grim-faced. Toni's gun ready in his hand. He had come to see that Bryce got an even chance when he and Quensel met.

'One . . . two. . . .'

Quensel fired at the count of two. Bryce felt the thudding hot pain in his shoulder. He squeezed the trigger of his gun just as Quensel shot a second time. Bryce's bullet tore a hole in the gambler's heart. Wade Applegate had fired at Quensel's gun hand, causing his second shot to go wild.

Pain shot from Bryce's shoulder down his arm to his fingertips. It hung numbed at his side as he walked towards the fallen gambler. When he made sure Quensel was dead, he followed Wade Applegate who had gone into the tepee and had lit a tallow dip candle.

Virginia Morgan lay stretched out on a tanned buffalo robe. Her eyelids were closed and her thin hands folded. A beautiful bride asleep. But it was the sleep of death. The buckhorn handle of a bowie knife, deep through her heart was almost hidden under her folded hands. Virginia Morgan lay cold, beautiful in death.

Quensel had been talking to the dead girl, whom he imagined had come as a ghost out of his past to haunt him.

Then Nile Carter was standing beside Bryce. She took the gun from his loose grip and shoved it into the empty holster of his thigh. Linking her arm through his, she led him back to her cottage.

Bryce sat straddle of the kitchen chair while Nile cut away his blood sodden shirt and undershirt with long bladed scissors. He flexed his fingers slowly, moving his arm from the shoulder socket. The bullet had ripped through the muscle, grazing the bone. There was no serious injury beyond the loss of blood and Nile worked in swift, sure silence to stop the crimson flow with gauze sponges and bandages.

Strangely, Bryce felt little pain. Only a dull, throbbing numbness. His eyes were dark with inward thoughts, remembering what Quensel had told about his back trail as he spewed out the slow poison that had been hidden deep within him during the long bitter years. Someday he'd tell Nile about it.

Wade Applegate came in and closed the door softly behind him. He told them that Virginia Morgan had taken her own life. She was dead when Quensel found her. He handed a paper to Nile. It was the agreement for the sale of the El Dorado which the gambler had signed before the midnight pay-off hour.

Nile told them that she'd met Big Tim

Fogarty after Bryce had left her and had told him he was welcome to the El Dorado. 'Tim never packed a gun', she said. 'His fists were his only weapon. He's never killed a man and never liked being tied up with Quensel and Kaster.'

Wade Applegate had brought Toni's money sack with him. He said he'd bank the money to the credit of Big Gregory and Marie, to give them a new start in life. He told Bryce that Virginia Morgan had left his money belt with Nile's squaw to give to him.

'I'm leaving for home now,' Wade Applegate said, looking kindly at them both. 'I'll have a buckboard waiting outside and I want you two to come to the ranch for a few days.'

When he had gone, Nile said they'd leave as soon as she signed over the El Dorado to Tim Fogarty.

'We're leaving Buffalo Run, Bryce, and we're never coming back.'

ABOUT THE AUTHOR

Walt Coburn was born in White Sulphur Springs, Montana Territory. He was once called "King of the Pulps" by Fred Gipson and promoted by Fiction House as "The Cowboy Author". He was the son of cattleman Robert Coburn, then owner of the Circle C ranch on Beaver Creek within sight of the Little Rockies. Coburn's family eventually moved to San Diego while still operating the Circle C. Robert Coburn used to commute between Montana and California by train and he would take his youngest son with him. When Coburn got drunk one night, he had an argument with his father that led to his leaving the family. In the course of his wanderings he entered Mexico and for a brief period actually became an enlisted man in the so-called "Gringo Battalion" of Pancho Villa's army.

Following his enlistment in the U.S. Army during the Great War, Coburn began writing Western short stories. For a year and a half he wrote and wrote before selling his first story to Bob Davis, editor of *Argosy-All Story*. Coburn married and moved to Tucson because his wife suffered from a respiratory condition. In a little adobe hut behind the main house Coburn practiced his art and for almost four decades he wrote approximately 600,000 words a year. Coburn's early fiction from his Golden Age — 1924–1940 — is his best, including his novels, *Mavericks* (1929) and *Barb Wire* (1931), as well as many short novels published only in magazines that now are being collected for the first time. In his Western stories, as Charles M. Russell and Eugene Manlove Rhodes, two men Coburn had known and admired in life, he captured the cow country and recreated it just as it was already passing from sight.

We hope you have enjoyed this Large Print book. Other Thorndike, Wheeler or Chivers Press Large Print books are available at your library or directly from the publishers.

For more information about current and upcoming titles, please call or write, without obligation, to:

Publisher
Thorndike Press
295 Kennedy Memorial Drive
Waterville, ME   04901
Tel. (800) 223-1244

Or visit our Web site at:
www.gale.com/thorndike
www.gale.com/wheeler

OR

Chivers Large Print
published by BBC Audiobooks Ltd
St James House, The Square
Lower Bristol Road
Bath BA2 3SB
England
Tel. +44(0) 800 136919
email: bbcaudiobooks@bbc.co.uk
www.bbcaudiobooks.co.uk

All our Large Print titles are designed for easy reading, and all our books are made to last.